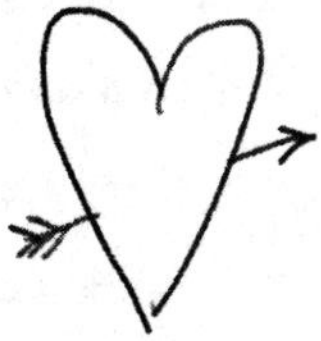

"Jake Gerhardt's debut novel is sweet, knowing, and a **super-fun read**. Takes you right back to the awkwardness and earnestness of adolescence, with a lot of cringe and even more laughs."

—PATTON OSWALT, *New York Times* bestselling author, comedian, and actor, on *Me & Miranda Mullaly*

MY FUTURE

EX-GIRLFRIEND

a novel by Jake Gerhardt

VIKING

VIKING
An imprint of Penguin Random House LLC
375 Hudson Street
New York, New York 10014

First published in the United States of America by Viking,
an imprint of Penguin Random House LLC, 2017

LIBRARY OF CONGRESS CATALOGING-IN-PUBLICATION DATA
Names: Gerhardt, Jake, date– author.
Title: My future ex-girlfriend / by Jake Gerhardt.
Description: New York : Viking, published by Penguin Group, [2017]. |
Summary: Amid worries about finals, commencement speeches,
and the baseball championship, eighth-graders Sam, Duke, and Chollie fumble
their way through being first-time boyfriends, hoping not to be dumped before
high school begins.
Identifiers: LCCN 2016027785 | ISBN 9780451475411 (hardback)
Subjects: | CYAC: Middle schools—Fiction. | Schools—Fiction. | Dating
(Social customs)—Fiction. | Humorous stories. | BISAC: JUVENILE FICTION /
Humorous Stories. | JUVENILE FICTION / Love & Romance. | JUVENILE FICTION
/ Social Issues / Emotions & Feelings.
Classification: LCC PZ7.1.G473 My 2017 | DDC [Fic]—dc23 LC record available
at https://lccn.loc.gov/2016027785

Printed in the USA   Decorations by Dana Li

1   3   5   7   9   10   8   6   4   2

This book is dedicated to my mother,
Nancy Gerhardt

"Boys are just like people, really."

—Booth Tarkington, *Penrod*

1

All Is Well

SAM

I'M THE FIRST guy at the bus stop, just waiting, waiting, waiting to get to Penn Valley Middle School. Part of me thinks I should just take off and start running, that's how excited I am. But before the adrenaline kicks in, I hear the bus rumbling as it turns the corner and approaches.

Once I'm on and seated, I just feel great, I really do. If we had a flat tire, I swear our bus driver, Ruben, wouldn't even have to jack up the bus. I could just lift it with one hand while he changed the tire. Are you getting the impression I'm excited for the final stretch of eighth grade to start?

You might be wondering why I'm so eager to get to school. The answer to that question is simple: Erica Dickerson, my new girlfriend. Erica is awesome and pretty. And pretty awesome. We got together just before spring break, and I spent most of my vacation thinking of all the things we'd get to do once we got back to school. Things like:

1. Double-date with my best friend, Foxxy, who hasn't been around as much since he started dating Holly Culver.
2. Sit together on the bus when we go to New York City for our end-of-the-year class trip. Oh, and hang out in the city, I guess.
3. Hang out at lunch together and have a civilized conversation instead of sitting around with the guys making fart sounds and putting butter on the floor to see if anyone slips.
4. Go to the eighth-grade dance! (I won't even mind if my sister's dumb boyfriend drives us.)

I can't wait to tell Foxxy about my plans.

When the bus pulls up to Foxxy's stop, I instantly get the feeling that something's wrong. I can't put my finger on it, it's just that Foxxy doesn't have a grin on his face. And he always grins. As I watch him get on the bus I'm hoping maybe he's just burped up his breakfast or something like that.

"Sam, Sam, Sammy," Foxxy says as he plops down on the seat next to me like it's the end of the day and not the beginning. "You're never going to believe what happened."

"What happened?"

"She did it, Sam. She really did it."

We fall back into our seat as Ruben takes off. He's an awesome bus driver, never in a bad mood. If he has to go to the bathroom, look out, our bus moves like a rocket. Today is one of those days.

"Who did what?" I ask.

"Holly. Holly did it," Foxxy says.

I look at Foxxy. His eyes are red and his nose is running. He looks like he hasn't slept in days. He's a mess.

"What did Holly do?"

"She dumped me, Sam. She dropped me like a bad habit."

Okay, so I don't want to be a jerk, but the first thing I think is that now we won't be able to double-date. And then I remember that Foxxy has a tendency to exaggerate.

"What did she say?" I ask.

"'I never want to see you again . . .'"

"It was probably in the heat of the moment."

"'. . . as long as I live,'" Foxxy says.

"That could be interpreted many different ways," I say, borrowing a line from my English teacher, Mr. Minkin. "Trust me. My sister Maureen breaks up with her boyfriend once a week."

And that's the truth. Maureen's in high school, and she goes out with this knucklehead (and I'm being generous here) named Lutz who's always doing something to make her upset.

"No, you don't understand," Foxxy continues. "She said it to my face. And then she sent me a text. And then I got an e-mail. And then she wrote me a letter, a real letter. And each time, she said she never wanted to see me again."

I look at Foxxy. Snot is dripping over his lips. His skin is pale and looks dry. His hair is uncombed. And his shirt is inside out. Besides that, he looks great.

"How could she honestly say she never wants to see you again?" I ask. "You look terrific. I'm sure she'll fall in love all over again when she takes one look at you."

Foxxy wipes his nose on his sleeve as the bus pulls up to school. Ruben jams on the breaks and leaps out of the door and sprints inside. I stand, ready to start my day.

"I think things will be fine. I'll see you at lunch, okay?"

"Where are you rushing off to?" Foxxy asks. "We still have fifteen minutes before class."

"I gotta see Erica," I say, running up the stairs to school.

"Hah," Foxxy says, right on my heels. "Is that still going on?"

"What do you mean, is that still going on?" I demand as we stop outside the cafeteria.

"I'm sorry. Look, I'm not myself. I can feel people staring at me. Everyone knows I got dumped."

And my mom says I'm dramatic. I put my hand on his shoulder, like a good best friend.

"I gotta go."

Then I skip off to see Erica. I actually skip, like one of those goofy kids from *The Sound of Music*. I'm actually smiling to myself, too, because I know if I saw someone skipping down the hall like this, I'd feel compelled to put a thumbtack on that person's seat. They'd totally deserve it.

Erica's locker is on the second floor near all the math classes. When I'm about two classrooms away, I see her. Wow. I mean, wow! Even though Mr. Minkin is always telling us to use descriptive adjectives in our writing, I don't know how to describe Erica besides saying she's a knockout. She's wearing a pink sweater and jeans and she looks just great in them. My heart is pounding like a hammer as I get near, and I've never felt better. I've got tunnel vision, and I'm really focused on Erica, and everything is a blur around her face. I feel like a superhero. I'm certain if someone came up to me and hit me on the back of the head with a wooden chair, the chair would splinter into a million pieces and it would only feel like a bug had flown into me.

The best part is that when Erica sees me, her eyes light up. They sparkle, and she gives me a great big smile.

She smiles like she is happy to see me.

She smiles like she missed me.

She smiles like I'm the most important person in the world.

"Hey, Sam," she says. It's the most romantic thing anyone has ever said to me.

And then:

"Hey, Foxxy. What are you two up to?"

I turn and see Foxxy right next to me. He's practically touching me, that's how close he is. He's so close I'm afraid his snot will drip on me.

"Just trying to keep it together today," Foxxy says, looking down at his sneakers.

Erica sticks her head in her locker to switch out some books, and I give Foxxy the old heave-ho with my thumb and whisper through my teeth, "Get out of here!"

"Didja hear, Erica, that I got dumped?" Foxxy asks, totally ignoring me.

"Oh no," Erica replies. "What happened?"

I'm the first guy to admit I don't know much about girls, but I do know this: girls love to hear about guys getting dumped by their girlfriends. My sisters spend hours on the phone talking about that kind of stuff. And when Foxxy gives Erica his sad eyes and pinches the top of his nose between his eyes like he's holding back tears, I know I'm in for the whole stupid, pathetic story again.

Foxxy tells Erica the whole stupid, pathetic story right there by her locker, and she listens to every word. Finally they stop talking, and Erica and I rush off to biology class, but we never get a chance to talk, and I never get a chance to tell her how much I missed her over break, and I never get a chance to ask if she missed me.

CHOLLIE

When I walk into Penn Valley Middle School after spring break, I'm a new man. A new man with a girlfriend. A girlfriend who picked me over other guys. It gives me this incredible feeling that I call the me-and-Miranda-Mullaly-dancing-in-the-moonlight feeling.

I haven't seen Miranda since we made it official before the break, because she went out of town. (I always forget where, but it's a state at the bottom of the US map.) She texted me a few times (seven times to be exact), which wasn't too much or too little. My older brother, Billy, who knows everything about girls, thinks that seven is the perfect number of texts. Too many, he says, and the girl could be trouble. Too few, and she's just not into you.

And because I miss her so much and this is, like, our one-week anniversary, I wrote her a letter last night. Here's what it says:

Dear Miranda,

This past week has been the best week of my life and I want you to know how happy I am that we're going out.

It's been a really great week even though you've been away visiting your grandparents and I've been here in Penn Valley thinking about you. When I think of your pretty smile I feel like I've just hit the winning shot or made a spectacular catch for a touchdown or hit a home run in the bottom of the ninth. I just feel great.

I miss you and will be so happy to see you in class.
Yours truly,
Charlie

So I have a big smile on my face, and I'm holding the letter like it's the most important thing in the world when I hear a voice.

"Are you ready, Chollie?"

It's Coach, who's an even bigger nut than I am about sports.

"Ready for what?" I ask Coach. Does he know about me and Miranda?

"Baseball," he says.

"I guess so," I say.

"Let's have a little chat," he says, and before I know it, Coach is leading me to his office.

His office is actually the office for all the gym teachers, but for some reason Coach always has it to himself. Sometimes I think he has the greatest job in the world. He gets to teach gym and coach football, basketball, and baseball. And he gets to wear a sweat suit to work every day.

"I think we're going to need you on the hill a few games this year," he says as he sits behind his desk, rubbing and sniffing a baseball.

"Okay," I say, and I sit down and take off my jacket and put down my book bag. I know once he gets going, I'll be here for a couple of minutes.

"Arms win championships, Chollie. The bats will come along, but we need pitching to win it all."

He gets up from behind his desk and writes the date May 20 on the board.

"Here's the big one, Chollie," he says, circling and underlining the date about a thousand times.

"You know what this date is?" he asks.

"It's the Cedarbrook game," I say.

Coach nods, and he doesn't have to say anything else. You see, Cedarbrook is our rival, and we lost to them in football when I fumbled on the goal line. And we lost to them in basketball when I missed those free throws at the end of the game.

Just the thought of those losses gets me interested in baseball again. I have to admit, I've been thinking so much about Miranda that baseball has kind of taken a backseat. But now I can picture myself striking out the side and then hitting a home run. And when I round third base, there's Miranda on her feet (for some reason, in my dream she's the only cheerleader wearing a fancy dress instead of a uniform) and cheering for me.

"So, Chollie, are you ready?" Coach asks again.

"I'll be ready," I say, and stand up. "But I also have to get to class," I tell him.

I rush off to class, and right outside the science room I get that me-and-Miranda-Mullaly-dancing-in-the-moonlight feeling again. My stomach is full of butterflies, and I feel like I could just float away. And then all at the same time I feel like everything is moving in slow motion and like there's no one else in the world except for me and Miranda. It's a pretty good feeling.

But since Coach keeps me, I don't have a chance to talk to Miranda before the bell rings. After class Miranda is already thinking about the final exam as I carry her book bag. Miranda is a lot like me, but instead of sports, Miranda is really into getting good grades and learning about all kinds of stuff.

I'm pretty sure she is happy to see me, but it's really hard to tell. You see, she's the kind of student who never says anything in class unless it's an answer to a question the teacher asks. Now that I think about it, I wonder if she's ever even asked to go to the bathroom. Amazing, right?

I walk her to her class, English, and I go off to history, and I don't get a chance to talk to Miranda until lunch when we meet in the library. And that's when a disaster strikes, and I lose that me-and-Miranda-Mullaly-dancing-in-the-moonlight feeling. In fact, I pretty much feel the way I felt when I lost the football and basketball championship games. I totally blow it.

DUKE

It was with a sense of purpose that I entered Penn Valley Middle School's benighted[1] halls to complete my final ten

----

1. Being in a state of moral or intellectual darkness; unenlightened.

weeks. Happily, however, I was in my own little world and soon to see Sharon Dolan, my new girlfriend. Our budding relationship had begun just a week earlier after we had finished starring in the spring musical, the only bright note in the otherwise desultory days of middle school.[2] I grinned thinking of her adorable smile, her innumerable talents (she sees and she observes!), her radiant eyes.

Yet before I even had a chance to greet my lady, who I hadn't seen because my parents forced me to join them at a conference in Boston, I discovered a note written on a Post-it stuck to my locker.

> *Duke—Come to my office when you get this!*
> *—Mr. Porter*

That note just about sums up this school. Mr. Porter, the student council sponsor, is a typical civil servant. He can tell you exactly when his next salary bump is scheduled but can't name a current member of Congress or a justice on the Supreme Court. Penn Valley is filled to the brim with his ilk, and a slack-jawed, ill-informed student body is the result.

....

2. I first fell for Sharon at the cast party I threw for my costars when she, to my great delight, quoted Sherlock Holmes. It was magic.

I ripped the Post-it from my locker, crumpled it in my fist, and made my way to the office.

The secretary ushered me directly into Mr. Lichtensteiner's office. Seated behind his desk and too lazy and ignorant to stand, he greeted me.

"Good morning, Mr. Samagura," he said.

I nodded and sized him up. Mr. Lichtensteiner is a modest man with a lot to be modest about.[3] It doesn't say much about Penn Valley that such a man rose to the great heights of vice principal.

"Please, sit down," he said.

"I prefer to stand," I said, then nodded in the direction of Mr. Porter, who was seated as if he were still on vacation.

"Very well. Let me tell it to you straight," Mr. Porter said. "We don't have the funds, nor do we have the manpower, to take the eighth grade on a class trip this year."

Mr. Porter tried to come off as upset, but he is a bad actor. It was grossly apparent to me that the bad news was in fact music to his ears. Mr. Porter sponsored the student council to pad his unearned paycheck, not because he cared to spend an extra minute with the students of Penn Valley.

I was shaken to the core, for I was very much looking

---

3. I'm paraphrasing Winston Churchill, who said of his political opponent Clement Attlee, "Mr. Attlee is a modest man. Indeed he has a lot to be modest about."

forward to this day away from Penn Valley. Mr. Porter, however, did not notice, for unlike him, I *can* act.

"I see," I said.

"As student council president, you're going to have to tell the student council tomorrow," Mr. Lichtensteiner said.

"This will come as quite a shock to the students, Mr. Lichtensteiner," I informed him.

"It most certainly will. I'm happy you're the one to tell them," Mr. Lichtensteiner said.

"What, exactly, am I expected to say?" I asked.

Mr. Porter looked up at me and handed me a paper. "Here's the e-mail from the school board. This details the reasons. Okay?"

I took the paper and scowled at it. Then I scowled at Mr. Lichtensteiner. I have never cared for this man, who has spent the last three years avoiding me like the plague, ignoring my warnings as the ship of Penn Valley Middle School was sinking.

"Good day, Mr. Samagura," Mr. Lichtensteiner said, picking up his phone.

But if he thought he was going to get rid of me quickly, he was sorely mistaken.

"I'd like to speak with someone higher up," I said.

Mr. Lichtensteiner looked at Mr. Porter, who shrugged his shoulders.

"I am as high up as this goes," Mr. Lichtensteiner said.

I heard the bell for class ring. And suddenly I knew I had missed Sharon. Since she's in the seventh grade, we don't have any classes together, and I really wanted to walk her to class.

"All right," I said. "Good day, sir."

I left Mr. Lichtensteiner's office thoroughly disappointed, but then it struck me like a bolt of lightning. Before Sharon entered my life, just about all I could think about was the class trip to New York City. But since Sharon is in the seventh grade and wouldn't be going on the class trip, I suddenly couldn't care less. We could go to the Big Apple by train and visit the Met[4] this summer. It was a relief knowing I wouldn't have to travel on a class trip to a cultural mecca like New York City with my uncouth classmates.

So it was with a careless, mirthful gait that I left the office that morning. In fact, I was close to skipping. I could hardly wait to see Sharon after school, especially since I would be taking the liberty of secretly decorating her locker to celebrate our one-week anniversary. Oh, to see the surprise in her lively blue eyes!

....

4. The world-famous Metropolitan Museum of Art in New York City. There is a very well-reviewed exhibition on view: *Pergamon and the Hellenistic Kingdoms of the Ancient World*.

2

All Is *Not* Well

DUKE

"SLOW DOWN," SHE said. Those were her exact words. Slow down.

I don't know "slow down." I don't do "slow down." It's not in my vocabulary.

And here I was expecting a big smile and a big hug and maybe even a little kiss. But instead, Sharon was embarrassed. Oh, I could tell. You don't go looking over your shoulders and searching for others' reactions if you're happy about something. No, you look right at the person who surprised you on your one-week anniversary as if that is the only person who exists. You don't care about anyone or anything else.

"You don't like balloons?" was all I could muster as a reply.

Sharon's initial shock left her face and her kind, empathetic smile returned.

"Oh, no, Duke, the balloons are sweet. It's just, perhaps, a bit too much."

There were only seven balloons tied to her locker. Seven. Was there a dearth[5] of balloons in the world of which I was unaware?

I was hurt, and though I pride myself on the ability to mask my feelings (practice for when I'm a lawyer and/or diplomat), Sharon, who is extraordinarily perceptive (she sees and she observes, don't forget[6]), could tell that I was taken aback. She put her hand on mine.

"I'm just surprised, that's all. We only got together a week ago. And . . ." She stopped there.

"And what?" I am by nature curious.

"It's just not something people do here at Penn Valley. Honestly, I'm just a little bit embarrassed, okay?"

This was the nightmarish memory that I could not rid from my mind as I sat down to dinner with my parents, Neal and Cassandra. If you don't know my parents, you're not missing much. They're both sociologists (hardly an

5. A scarce supply; lack; shortage.

6. From Sherlock Holmes. Sharon and I both very much enjoy these classic mysteries from the pen of Sir Arthur Conan Doyle.

intellectually invigorating field) and allegedly teach at the town's poor excuse for a college, Penn Valley College, and write useless books together. They recently completed a book, *Ethel's Story*,[7] which I perused and had no choice but to give two thumbs down. They do stay busy and usually don't have time for me, which is fine. Recently they've been rallying their students to protest at Penn Valley College. About what, your guess is as good as mine.

Anyway, here's an example of our tedious dinner conversation:

SCENE ONE[8]

LIGHTS UP

THE DINING ROOM of the Samagura residence in Penn Valley, a suburb of Philadelphia. DUKE, fourteen, handsome, sits at the table between his parents, NEAL and CASSANDRA. The stage is well lit, bright on the table.

(They eat in silence.)

....

7. The third book in their vapid series on the Voiceless in America.

8. I intend to write a couple of plays to improve the current wasteland known as Broadway after I graduate from Princeton with a degree in international relations. Since Sharon is a natural and talented thespian. I'll give her the starring roles, of course.

Cassandra

How is your little friend?

Duke

She's not my "little friend." She is the
same size as any average seventh-grader.

Cassandra

How is your friend?

Duke

Quite well, thank you. I trust she had a
relaxing spring break and is refreshed for
the final ten weeks of the school year.

*(There is a distinct pause here. Then Neal coughs
and begins.)*

Neal

Is there nutmeg in the soup?

Cassandra

There shouldn't be nutmeg.

Neal

I distinctly taste nutmeg.

(They return to their soups.)

Cassandra

Duke, do you taste nutmeg?

Duke

Maybe.

Cassandra

That's curious. There shouldn't be any nutmeg.

Neal

I could be wrong.

Cassandra

No, if you say you taste it, there must be some in there. Perhaps I made a mistake. I'll have to reorganize the spice rack.

Neal

I'll help you.

Cassandra

Thank you, dear.

(*Cassandra and Neal mouth I love you.*)

Duke

May I be excused?

Cassandra

Already? *Pourquoi?*[9]

Duke

I'm going to vomit.

FADE TO BLACK

Do you see what I have to work with? Oh, what I would give to witness my parents have a little tiff or kerfuffle. I blame them for my balloon faux pas.

Sitting at my desk with a spot of tea, I did all I could to concentrate on my duties as a student and leader in the school. The next ten weeks will be the busiest of my life, and it's going to take a great deal of skill to juggle my relationship with Sharon with my many responsibilities. As

....
9. "Why" in French. *Brava*, Cassandra!

president of the student council, it falls upon me to plan almost every activity my thankless peers will enjoy as their middle-school years come to an end. In fact, I'm probably busier than the president of the United States.[10]

I moved over to my coziest chair and settled in with Shakespeare's sonnets. It helped put my mind at ease.

SAM

"How's your future ex-girlfriend?"

"Huh?" I say, looking over at my sister Maureen's boyfriend, John Lutz. He's a sophomore at Penn Valley High and an all-around jerk. Who needs an older brother picking on you when you have a guy like Lutz hanging around the house?

"I asked," he repeats, and much slower, like I'm an idiot or something, "how's your future ex-girlfriend, Erica?" Lutz laughs like he just made a joke, but I certainly don't think it's funny.

I don't bother answering Lutz. First of all, what's he even doing at our dinner table? My mom doesn't ask if he's staying anymore, she just sets an extra space at the table.

"Leave him alone," Maureen says, sticking up for me

10. You can see the president's schedule on whitehouse.gov/schedule. It looks to me like the American taxpayer is getting ripped off once again.

for the first time ever. "I think it's cute our little Sammy has a girlfriend."

So much for sticking up for me. Even though she's only a year older, she makes me feel like a little kid and I don't like it. And then there's my younger sister, Sharon, who treats me the same way, even though she's in the seventh grade.

Mom puts a plate of food in front of Lutz (can you believe he gets served first?—my dad notices), but at least that shuts him up.

Everyone starts eating and talking, but I just can't get my mind off of how annoying Foxxy was today. He talked to Erica all through lunch and then after school. When I walked up to them, Erica was giving Foxxy relationship advice. He talked to her more than I did!

And I'm in my own world, I really am, until we're done with dinner. I look at my plate and it's empty, though I don't remember eating. Then my mom serves us ice cream for dessert and that's when Lutz farts.

"Jesus, Sam, what was that?" he asks.

I'm too shocked to say anything. I mean, who farts at the dinner table and then blames someone else? Lutz, that's who. And you'd think my mom would know it was Lutz and wouldn't tolerate him swearing (sort of) at the dinner table, but God forbid someone takes my side. Here's how it plays out:

Sharon: Oh my gosh, you're so gross!

Maureen: I'm so ashamed and embarrassed!

Mom: Excuse yourself, Sam.

Dad: Is there more chocolate ice cream?

Even though I feel the way my dad does, I just get up from the table and go to my room. And anyway, I have to figure out what to do about Foxxy.

As I stare at my fish tank it occurs to me that Lutz, who's a total idiot, might just be right about something. Erica is going to be my future ex-girlfriend if I don't play my cards right. I'll start high school girlfriendless, spending Friday nights at the movies sharing popcorn with Foxxy.

CHOLLIE

I can't sleep.

I'm lying in bed and I'm wide-awake. Every time I close my eyes I see it, just sitting there in Coach's office. A light blue envelope with "Miranda" written on the front. I just can't get the picture of the letter I wrote for Miranda out of my head.

The worst part of forgetting the letter in Coach's office is that Miranda remembered it was our one-week anniversary.

Here's what happens. I meet Miranda at the library during lunch. She likes to go there a lot, and when we were working on our report on the Brazilian tapir (before we were boyfriend and girlfriend), we had "working lunches" three times a week. So of course I can't wait for lunch today, not only because I'm pretty much starving by lunchtime, but also because it's the first chance I get to really talk to Miranda all day.

I'm waiting and waiting, but she's not there, so I figure she's probably talking to a teacher or something, and this gives me a chance to eat my awesome turkey sandwich. No one can make a sandwich like my mom. And all I think about is how great the sandwich is and how great it will be to see Miranda, especially when I give her the letter I wrote.

Miranda arrives and I can tell right away she's upset about something. It almost looks like she's been crying.

"Charlie," she says, "you'll never believe what has happened."

Isn't it cool how Miranda calls me Charlie? Everyone else calls me Chollie because I couldn't say Charlie in kindergarten. Isn't that stupid? But I like that everyone calls me Chollie and only Miranda calls me Charlie.

"What happened?" I ask.

"We're not going to have our eighth-grade class trip."

"Why not?"

"We didn't raise enough money and the school board is making cuts."

"That's okay," I tell her. I think about reaching out and touching her hand but decide against it. "What's the big deal about a class trip anyway?" I ask, trying to make her feel better.

"Don't you want to go to New York?" she asks.

"Sure, I guess, but I always get a little carsick on the bus. And whenever we're on class trips, it always feels like we're rushing around just so we can get back on time."

"I feel, I don't know, like I failed when I was the student council president. I should have never resigned after the toilet paper incident."

"You did a great job," I tell her, and I still think about holding her hand, but I don't.

"I guess we'll figure out something else," she says, and even though she smiles, she doesn't seem totally convinced. "Oh, I almost forgot. I have something for you."

She digs into her backpack and takes out a card. "Happy one-week anniversary," she says.

It all happens so fast. I open the card and it's a picture from the book *Goodnight Moon*, which was my favorite book as a kid. I can't believe she remembered! Inside is written "Happy one-week anniversary! XOXO Miranda."

I look at Miranda and give her a big, huge smile.

"I know it's corny," she says, "but I couldn't resist. My ex-boyfriend, Tom, and I used to do stuff like this. I thought it was fun to remember the little things."

"Oh, sure, yeah, it's great," I say. And before I know it, I have my book bag up on the table and I'm searching for the letter.

"I have a letter for you in here somewhere," I say.

I'm really frantic, looking for that letter.

"It's okay, Charlie, really it is."

"I didn't forget it," I say. "I swear."

And now I'm sweating and I have everything out of my bag.

"I believe you," she says.

Thankfully, the bell rings, and I can tell Miranda is happy to get out of the library.

I watch her leave, and then the image of that dumb letter comes into my head.

And it's still in my head now, and every time I close my eyes to go to sleep I see it, just sitting there on Coach's office floor, with "Miranda" written on it.

3

What's on Deck

DUKE

EVERY HERO HAS an enemy. Othello had Iago; Hamlet had Fate; Sherlock Holmes had Professor Moriarty.[11] Yours truly has Ralph Waldo.

He was waiting for me in the lobby of the auditorium, swaying on the crutches he has been carrying about ever since his skiing accident.

"Hello, Duke," Ralph Waldo said. "What say you?"

"Ralph," I said. "I hope your leg is healing."

"It is indeed, Duke. Thank you for asking. And how are things with the charming Sharon Dolan?"

"Splendid, Ralph. Thank you for asking." I really enjoyed

---

11. Earlier in the semester Chollie Muller and Sam Dolan were my enemies over a now-forgotten matter.

saying this. I was happy to rub it in Ralph's face. And knowing Knuckles and Moose[12] were cracking their knuckles in their pinstripe suits and homburgs,[13] waiting to inflict pain on Ralph, made me even happier.

"Quite the catch you reeled in, Duke."

Ralph returned my blissful smile with an evil grin. I knew instantly I was no longer dealing with your run-of-the-mill eighth-grader but instead beheld my Iago, my Fate, my Professor Moriarty. Not just a competitor, like the now-vanquished Sam and Chollie, but a man who would stop at nothing to get what he wanted.

"Ta-ta," I said, touching his shoulder in a most condescending way as I entered the empty auditorium to prepare for my duties.

I quickly put Ralph Waldo out of my mind, for I had more important things with which to deal. Not only was the student council going to get the bad news that there would be no class trip, but the meeting was to be more crowded than usual, since we needed volunteers to serve on committees for the various end-of-the-year activities, the most important being the eighth-grade dance.

....

12. Don't laugh. Knuckles and Moose are my imaginary friends who keep me in good form while also keeping my enemies in line.

13. Hats commonly worn by most men in a better time. After I've reintroduced the bow tie to the world, I may wear a fedora or homburg.

And to make matters worse, I was terribly worried about Sharon. She should not be wallowing in the seventh grade, working on simple algebra, reading whatever tripe the school district is forcing students to read, wasting her time overall. I wouldn't be able to see her angelic face all day.

Mr. Porter was the first to enter the auditorium and called my name upon seeing me. He was especially nervous, and although I wasn't as worried as he, I really didn't want to tell the eighth-graders the bad news. Still, it was my job, so I would do it.

I assuaged Mr. Porter's fears. "As we discussed, I'll handle this."

The good thing about an incompetent nincompoop like Mr. Porter is that he listens to me. He took a seat and began a crossword, which he could never possibly finish.

The auditorium filled up quickly. I was so happy to see Sharon enter, her eyes focusing upon mine as she walked down the aisle. She was a ray of light in the dark hall.

"Ladies and gentlemen," I began. "I have some disappointing news. There will be no eighth-grade class trip."

I must admit I was not expecting the student council to take the bad news the way they did. But after years of constant disappointment, a below-average faculty with low expectations, and dispiriting losses in sports to Cedarbrook, I suppose the student body at Penn Valley has come to expect the worst. In fact, after an initial groan of disappointment, the students, led by Miranda Mullaly and seconded by the pulchritudinous[14] Sharon Dolan, began planning an alternate activity.

Before I knew it, they were discussing some nonsense about bringing New York City to Penn Valley and having a talent show to raise funds for an undetermined and undeserving charity. It sounded better to me than taking a dirty yellow school bus to New York City, especially since Sharon wouldn't be with me.

I moved on and ran the meeting quite smoothly and professionally. (Mr. Porter should have been taking notes to see how it is done but instead slumbered in the corner.) We began to split up into smaller groups so I could delegate many of the responsibilities and be more efficient. I asked for volunteers for the various committees, and they were filling up quickly.

"One of our last committees will be," I said, looking down at my notes to get it correct, "the spirit committee. This committee will be responsible for building up excitement

....
14. Characterized by or having great physical beauty and appeal.

for the event." When I looked up from my notes, I saw Sharon's glorious smile and her hand waving bravely. I lovingly pointed to her.

"Great. Sharon Dolan."

And then one more hand, the hand of the treacherous, the lecherous, the insidious Ralph Waldo. I ignored him.

"Now for our next order of business—" I started, but was rudely interrupted by Ralph.

"Excuse me, but I would like to volunteer for the spirit committee."

"It's been filled," I said nonchalantly, then looked down at my papers and pretended to write something.

"By whom?" Ralph Waldo called out shooting up on his feet.

"Excuse me?" I said.

"Who has filled the position for the spirit committee? I only saw Sharon Dolan's hand go up."

"I am going to be on that committee as well," I explained. "So you see, the position is filled."

Ralph Waldo refused to take his seat and yelled, "Point of order! Point of order!"

His shouting woke Mr. Porter.

"What now, Ralph?" Mr. Porter asked.

"It is clear that the president will not serve on a committee but will oversee the committees' work. That is the main role of the chief executive," Ralph explained.

"What are you saying, Ralph?" Mr. Porter asked.

"I want to be on the spirit committee," he said.

"Fine." Mr. Porter sighed. "Duke, please put Ralph on the spirit committee."

"Of course," I grumbled.

Ralph returned to his seat with a triumphant grin. But it wouldn't last long, for within seconds Knuckles and Moose descended upon him for a good old-fashioned thrashing. Mr. Porter was next in line for an attitude adjustment. He would've been better off sleeping through the meeting rather than meddling in my affairs.

CHOLLIE

When I get to school this morning, I go right to Coach's office, and sitting there on the floor is the letter I wrote to Miranda. Boy, am I lucky no one visits Coach and that he never cleans his office.

Of course I have to stick around and talk to Coach for a bit, and when I get to science class, Mrs. Stempen is already teaching, even though the bell hasn't rung yet. So I don't have a chance to give Miranda the letter, and the more I think about it, I figure maybe I should just give up on it. I also have a problem remembering dates, so I'm not sure what date I wrote on the letter. And if I put the wrong date, Miranda might think I was lying yesterday. It certainly isn't easy having a girlfriend.

At lunch I sit with Miranda and her friends in the cafeteria. They're very excited about the end of the year. And there are so many events that we're going to be super busy. I hardly get a chance to talk, which is fine with me because I really don't understand all the stuff Miranda and her friends are talking about.

I walk Miranda to class after lunch, keeping my hand near the letter in my back pocket.

"Thanks for walking me to class, Charlie," Miranda says. "I'll see you at the student council meeting right after school."

"Okay."

I can't wait for the final bell to ring. When it does, I run off for the meeting. Miranda is waiting for me outside the auditorium, and we walk in together.

The meeting starts as soon as we take our seats. Duke Samagura, this pretty uptight guy who might have had a crush on Miranda at one point, tells everyone that the eighth-grade class trip has been canceled because of insufficient funds. There's sort of some groaning, but that's about it. And then Miranda takes over.

First, Miranda stands. And then she waits. When the

groaning stops, she speaks. It's something to see, let me tell you. It's like when Stephen Curry has a hot hand and you just know you can't stop him.

First she asks, "If we can't go to New York City, why don't we bring New York City to us?"

Everyone is quiet.

"I mean, what do they have in New York City?"

I don't think anyone has an answer to that. I can only think of the Knicks and Yankees and Mets. And it's not like we were going to see them on our class trip. And the Giants and Jets play in New Jersey, and we weren't going to New Jersey.

I guess everyone is thinking like me, that there's really nothing in New York City.

Finally someone yells out, "Art exhibits!"

"We'll have an art exhibit here, but the work will be by Penn Valley students."

Sam Dolan yells out, "Comedy clubs!"

"We'll make our own comedy club here. And the entertainment will be Penn Valley students."

Someone else yells out, "Broadway shows!"

"We'll do it better here. But with . . ."

And everyone shouts, "Penn Valley students!"

And does Miranda really get on a roll after that. She takes over the meeting, and suddenly, everyone is shouting out ideas. Pretty soon everyone volunteers to help, and it's decided tickets will be sold to raise money not for the school but for some wonderful cause, like starving children or refugees or something like that.

Before we know it, we're going to have the entire school and community there!

It's awesome sitting there and watching my girlfriend get everyone all excited to work together. It's kind of like she's a coach and we're her team. Then I remember that I have a real coach and I'm late for baseball tryouts. And even though Coach yells at me, I'm still thinking about Miranda the whole time.

SAM

If you know anything about Penn Valley, you know that Mr. Lichtensteiner is the vice principal and he takes his job very seriously. His mission in life, it seems to me, is to keep the student body from having any fun.

It's the first week after spring break and Lichtensteiner has got ants in his pants again. You'd think he'd be relaxed after spring break, but not him!

He stops me after school on the way to the student council meeting.

"Where are you going, Dolan?" he asks, and I can see he has recently eaten a granola bar.

"I'm going to the student council meeting. If you'll excuse me, I'm running a little late."

"You're not on the student council."

It really burns me up when Lichtensteiner acts like he knows everything about me. It's true I'm not officially on the student council, but a bunch of us are volunteering for the end-of-the-year activities. God forbid Lichtensteiner know that.

"I am today," I say, and walk around the big lunk.

"Listen here, Dolan," he says. "I know Foxxy got dumped by Holly Culver. I'll be watching you two very closely, very closely. Got it?"

Does this man have problems or what? I think he's still upset about the toilet paper incident. That was when he decided to take all the toilet paper out of the boys' bathrooms because someone was throwing wet toilet paper on the walls. I led the rebellion to get our toilet paper back, and the whole thing culminated in me bursting into a student council meeting to give a speech about how toilet paper is a right. Lichtensteiner isn't the kind of guy to forget something like that. But this afternoon I just keep on walking toward the auditorium.

The room is pretty crowded, but Erica has a seat saved and she waves me over. Just as I'm about to sit down, Foxxy snags it, so I have to sit behind them.

I lean forward to say hello, but Foxxy is already talking Erica's ear off.

"What's she doing with him?" he asks Erica as he points to Holly just a few rows ahead of us.

"I don't think they came in together," Erica says, trying to reassure him.

"Forget about it, Foxxy," I say, and even though I feel like Lutz for saying it, I add, "besides, there's plenty of fish in the ocean."

Erica looks back at me, and she's shocked. She's really shocked.

"Wow, Mr. Sensitivity." Then she puts her hand on Foxxy's shoulder. The hand that should be on my shoulder. The hand that should be in my hand. "Would you say that about us if we were in this situation?"

Foxxy and Erica both look at me, waiting for the answer. That's when I notice my sister Sharon is sitting next to Erica, and she looks back and she's waiting for an answer, too.

I figure I'm better off just leaning back and listening to what everyone has to say. But I tell you this, I'm getting sick of Foxxy palling around with my girl. And I'm always sick of Sharon.

The meeting finally starts, and Duke (a total dork) tells us we're not going on a class trip. Then everyone starts talking about having some kind of big talent show instead. And I shout out we should have a comedy stage, and everyone thinks it's a good idea. But I can't stick around too long because we have tryouts for the baseball team. I say good-bye to Erica and she promises she'll get us on a good committee together.

When I get up to go, Foxxy and Erica look back at me.

"Bye," Erica says.

"We'll be sure to get you on a committee with us," Foxxy adds.

Okay, so all that is typical. But you'll never guess what happens next. As I'm walking toward the locker room, I start thinking about the meeting. And then I really start to think about this talent show. And then I walk right past the locker room and out the door and walk all the way home, completely blowing off baseball tryouts.

The entire time I'm thinking about this talent show. Can you imagine how much fun a talent show would be with everybody doing something and then having me come out, make comments on the previous act, and then introduce the next one? I can even write some skits for me and Erica to perform.

But before I get to that, I have got to figure out what to do with Foxxy. If I don't get rid of him soon, I'll never have a chance to be alone with Erica, let alone emcee a talent show with her.

So here's my five-point plan of attack:

1. Find Foxxy a new girlfriend. That shouldn't be too hard, since obviously Holly Culver used to see something in him.

2. Keep Foxxy busy. I'll talk Foxxy into signing up for a lot of committees.

3. Spend some time helping Foxxy get his act together. Tomorrow teach him how to use a fork and knife at lunch, and we'll talk about his personal hygiene.

4. Get Foxxy back together with Holly Culver (if first plan doesn't work). Maybe when she said she never wanted to see him again, she was overexaggerating.

5.

Okay, so I have a four-point plan, but it's a start.

4
Freewriting

Duke Vanderbilt Samagura

1 April 2016

English 8A

Mr. Minkin

Suggested Writing Prompt: *With only ten weeks left until commencement, your years at Penn Valley Middle School are coming to an end. Write about either what you have accomplished in the last three years or what you want to accomplish in the last ten weeks. Or both!*

Sir:

A more apt question would be what have <u>you</u> accomplished? You, Mr. Minkin, who have wasted numerous hours with your "freewriting"? You and your superficial interpretations of literature, which obviously come directly from the textbook or whatever you can find on the Internet. What have you accomplished? Very little, I must say.

I, on the other hand, have accomplished a great deal at this school. Indeed, Penn Valley Middle will be the worse for it when I move on to Penn Valley High.

I have:

- Starred in the school's production of <u>The Pajama Game</u>, single-handedly improving the integrity of our theatre department
- Stepped up to the plate to lead our school as the student council president after Miranda Mullaly's resignation
- Assembled an awesome yearbook
- Won the heart of the delightful Sharon Dolan

I will:

- Add the finishing touches on the eighth-grade dance

- Figure out how to put on NYC Nights in less than nine weeks
- Finish up strong to win the not-very-prestigious top grades award
- Write and give an unforgettable commencement speech
- Keep an eye on Ralph Waldo
- And of course enjoy and savor these last ten weeks here with Sharon Dolan, the beacon of light in the benighted world of Penn Valley Middle School

Pretty daunting, isn't it, Mr. Minkin? Aren't you glad you're an indolent English teacher instead of Duke Vanderbilt Samagura?

Sam Dolan

April 1st 2016

English 8A

Mr. Minkin

Suggested Writing Prompt: *With only ten weeks left until commencement, your years at Penn Valley Middle School are coming to an end. Write about either what you have accomplished in the last three years or what you want to accomplish in the last ten weeks. Or both!*

Hey Mr. Minkin,

Cool question. It's hard to believe we're in the final ten weeks. Doesn't graduation seem really far away but also really close at the same time? Freaky if you think about it. It's sort of like waiting and waiting for Christmas and then you blink and it's January and you're back in school.

I don't think I've accomplished much in the three years other than getting a girlfriend. I mean, the toilet paper rebellion isn't really an accomplishment. And starting a fire (by accident!) in the science lab is not an accomplishment either, even if people were happy the school was evacuated and we were on the news.

So instead I will concentrate on the next ten weeks. And what an exciting ten weeks they will be. Here's my plan:

1. Get rid of Foxxy. I started on this today by showing him how to use a fork and knife during lunch. He only ate half of his lunch (spaghetti) with his fingers.

2. Take Erica Dickerson to the eighth-grade dance and figure out how to get a ride so someone other than my parents drives us. (Maybe her dad's a nice guy and wouldn't mind giving us a ride?)

3. Figure out something awesome to do for the talent show. I'm thinking Erica and I should do some kind of sketch comedy like on *Key and Peele*.

There are some other things I should add, like keeping my nose clean and avoiding Lichtensteiner. And I guess I should stay on top of my classwork and all that.

There's so much to do I'm just about ready to jump out of my seat and get started.

Wow, Mr. Minkin. I mean, wow!

Chollie Muller
April 1, 2016
English 8A
Mr. Minkin

Suggested Writing Prompt: *With only ten weeks left until commencement, your years at Penn Valley Middle School are coming to an end. Write about either what you have accomplished in the last three years or what you want to accomplish in the last ten weeks. Or both!*

Dear Mr. Minkin,

If you would've asked me this question a couple of weeks ago I would have been depressed answering it. I was going around constantly worried and nervous, trying to remember my one line and dance moves for the school play and feeling pressured about how to ask out Miranda Mullaly. It sure wasn't easy.

Now that that's behind me I'm feeling pretty good, though I can't say I've really accomplished anything. But that's all right, because like you say, we have ten weeks to go.

What I would like to accomplish is to win

the baseball championship and not mess up like I did during the football and basketball championship games. We were so close and I was the one who was in position to secure victory. Can you imagine fumbling when you're going in for <u>the</u> touchdown or missing a game-winning free throw? It's a really terrible feeling.

So baseball is totally what I'm looking forward to and winning the championship trophy and then putting it in the trophy case and coming back to see it. I could even bring my kids here (when I have kids) and show them the trophy. Now that would be a totally awesome accomplishment.

Top it all off by going to the eighth-grade dance with Miranda and I'll feel like I accomplished everything I've dreamed of.

Miranda Mullaly

April 1, 2016

English 8A

Mr. Minkin

Suggested Writing Prompt: *With only ten weeks left until commencement, your years at Penn Valley Middle School are coming to an end. Write about either what you have accomplished in the last three years or what you want to accomplish in the last ten weeks. Or both!*

I can't believe there are only ten weeks left in the year. It seems like just a few weeks ago I felt there was nothing at Penn Valley I'd miss. But now that Charlie and I are a couple, I suddenly feel there are many things I will miss. Isn't that strange?

Before Charlie (B.C.?) I would have just thought about grades and being on the student council as accomplishments, but now, I don't know, they just don't seem to matter as much.

I also don't want to look back because there are a few things I find a little embarrassing. I don't want to look back on how rotten I felt

when my ex, Tom Nelson, broke up with me.
What did I see in him? Why did I even care?

And I don't want to look back on the day
I resigned as student council president. It
was rash to get so angry about a toilet paper
rebellion but at that moment in my life I was not
one to be amused by high jinks. If that happened
today I would laugh with everyone else. And
that's all thanks to Charlie.

So what do I want to accomplish for the last
ten weeks?

I want to do everything possible to make the
eighth-grade dance a huge success. I want to
finish strong in all my classes. And I want to put
together an amazing alternative to the canceled
class trip (boohoo), NYC Nites. Not only will
NYC Nites be great fun but it will also raise
money and awareness for a great cause (still
haven't nailed down a specific cause but we're
open to suggestions!).

And the best part is that I'll be able to do this
with Charlie as my boyfriend!

Erica Dickerson

April 1, 2016

English 8A

Mr. Minkin

Suggested Writing Prompt: *With only ten weeks left until commencement, your years at Penn Valley Middle School are coming to an end. Write about either what you have accomplished in the last three years or what you want to accomplish in the last ten weeks. Or both!*

If having fun, Mr. Minkin, could be considered an accomplishment, then that's what I plan on doing in the next ten weeks. And how could I not have fun? Hanging with Sam is like a day at an amusement park, but without the popcorn, soda, and roller coasters.

I'm so glad Sam and I are a couple. Every morning Sam makes my day when he greets me at my locker and it's always so exciting hanging with him and his friends. Today at lunch Sam and Foxxy practically had me on the floor from laughing as Sam (of all people) tried to show Foxxy how to eat properly. They're like a comedy team, those two, they really are.

But I sort of feel bad for Foxxy, who just got dumped by Holly Culver. The poor guy is really broken up over it. I've been trying to include him in everything Sam and I are doing so he doesn't feel as lonely. (Sam thinks Foxxy should try to get back together with Holly, but trust me. It ain't happening.)

Fortunately there are plenty of things to distract him with, like the dance, graduation, and NYC Nites. I'm going to make sure Foxxy is with us as we put together all the end-of-the-year activities. He may not appreciate it, but I'm sure Sam will.

Okay, that's it for now. Here's to the next ten weeks. We're going to have a blast! And don't forget to buy your tickets for NYC Nites!!

5

NYC Nites It Is

CHOLLIE

The best thing about having your girlfriend practically in charge of running the school is that you get all the information about what's happening before anyone else. Sometimes our meetings in the library are like scenes out of *Law & Order*, Billy's favorite show, when the one guy tells all the detectives what to do.

So today at lunch I can see when she comes into the library there's something wrong.

"Bad news?" I ask as she takes a seat.

"News is news," she says. "It's only bad news if we let it be bad news."

It's amazing how optimistic she is, right? She'd be a

perfect baseball player, never letting a bad at bat get in the way. I should really be writing this stuff down. She could make millions on a self-help book. I know Billy would buy a couple of copies.

"What is it?" I ask, unwrapping my second turkey, cheese, and bacon sandwich. Miranda takes a long look at it, and I'm not sure if I should offer her a bite or not. Billy doesn't think sharing food is a good idea this early in the relationship.

"I just met with Mr. Lichtensteiner, Mr. Porter, and Duke. We can't have the dance and NYC Nites. We have to choose one or the other."

I'm speechless. And not because I'm shocked, but more because I really don't understand how all this stuff works.

"We have to decide by the end of the day." Then she asks, "Which would you rather do?"

"I don't know," I say. "I really wanted to go to the dance with you, but the thought of everybody getting together for NYC Nites seems like it would be super fun, too. I wish we could do both."

Miranda smiles. "Me too. But I guess we'll find out soon enough."

She starts on her work and I pretend to read my history book.

"Oh, Charlie, there's something I forgot to ask you," Miranda says.

"What's that?"

"Would you like to have dinner with me and my parents Sunday night?"

Have you ever had the wind knocked out of you? It doesn't hurt, but it's really scary because you can't breathe. That's how I feel: just like I've been punched in the gut.

"This Sunday?"

"If you're free," Miranda says.

I don't know if you heard about what happened at the Mullaly residence after Valentine's Day, but it wasn't pretty. Duke, Sam, and I all had the same idea of shoveling the snow off Miranda's sidewalk and it ended with Mr. Mullaly's car window smashed and him chasing us down the street in his underwear because he was too mad to remember to put on pants. It's all pretty embarrassing and I know my face is getting red just thinking about it.

"Are you still worried about the snow day?" Miranda asks.

Amazing. She can read minds, too!

I can only nod.

"It's okay," Miranda says, and then reaches out and touches my hand. And you know what? It is okay. It's like magic. And when she says it's going to be okay and she touches my hand and smiles I get my breath back and feel 100 percent better.

I feel so good I finish my sandwich in one bite.

SAM

I'm a man on a mission Monday morning. I'm going to get Foxxy a girlfriend. First on my list is Terri McCool.

Me: Hi, Terri.

Terri: Hi, Sam.

Me: Have you heard about Foxxy and Holly Culver?

Terri: Yeah. I can't believe it took so long for Holly to dump him.

Me: What do you mean?

Terri: I mean, what did she ever see in him? He wears the same clothes all the time and acts like he's in kindergarten. And once we counted him wiping his nose with his hand a total of seventeen times until we simply had to stop counting.

I cross Terri's name off the list.

I forget about Terri pretty fast, as a rumor goes around that we can't have NYC Nites *and* the eighth-grade dance. According to the rumor, we're going to vote on one or the other after school. I'm really looking forward to both, but then at lunch it hits me as I watch Foxxy slurping his chili from a bowl and telling Erica a stupid story about Holly that there's no way Foxxy is going to have a date for the dance. I make up my mind.

For the first time since the toilet paper rebellion, I give a passionate speech at a student council meeting.

"What's the big deal about an eighth-grade dance?" I ask. "Every school has an eighth-grade dance, but NYC Nites, that's unique. I say we vote for that!"

Don't get me wrong, I was really excited about the dance, even though I don't have a suit and I was probably going to have to get a ride from either my father or Lutz. But when the choice is between a big event where Foxxy could get lost or a dance where he'd likely be a third wheel, it was a simple choice for me. Anyway, our dances tend to be pretty boring. The Valentine's Day dance was just about the worst night of my life. The girl I sort of liked wasn't there, and I ended up eating pizza by myself and hiding in the bathroom. Like I said, worst night of my life.

After I speak no one else says anything and we have the vote. I guess a lot of people feel like I do. No, that's not right. Most people don't care and don't vote. So first place was no vote and second place was NYC Nites. It's not a landslide, but a win's a win.

When it's all settled and Duke makes it official by hammering his gavel—yes, he actually has a gavel, like he's a judge or something—Erica and I grab the back table in the auditorium where the teachers sit as they try to stay awake during study group. Just as we're about to get to work—and don't think for a second writing sketch comedies is easy—Foxxy comes over and sits down between us.

"What are you doing here?" I ask, hoping he can hear from my tone that we're busy.

"I can't work with the food committee. Julie Singer is there."

"What's wrong with that?" I say.

"Julie Singer and Holly are friends. I just can't be in a group with her," he says.

I'm not a stickler for rules, but I think Foxxy volunteered for the food committee, and if he changes groups, then suddenly everyone will be doing whatever they jolly well please and the whole school will fall apart. There'd be chaos. I'm about to tell this to Foxxy when Erica says:

"Oh, that must be hard on you. You can work with us."

And that's the story of how Foxxy spent the afternoon and then the rest of the week with me and Erica on the entertainment committee.

We work right at that table after school, going through

our ideas, getting the volunteers for our acts, figuring out if we'll have tryouts.

Here's a couple of things that we have so far:

- A talent stage for stand-up comedy (me and Erica), singing, dancing, juggling, etc.
- An art gallery that we'll set up in Ms. Kerrigan's room, which fortunately is right next to the auditorium.

Okay, so it's only two things. But it did take us a long time to get these ideas hammered out. And Miranda and Mr. Porter think they're good ideas. Even Duke, the kind of guy who would frown at a pot of gold, thinks it's a great idea.

But the best part of the whole week comes on Thursday. Erica and I are working on the auditorium stage, trying to figure out how we're going to entertain the crowd on the big night. When we're alone backstage, going through the backdrops for the scenery, Erica gets really quiet, and I can tell she's not thinking about NYC Nites.

"What are you doing on Sunday?" Erica asks, and she is real nonchalant about it. But I can also hear in her voice, which goes a little higher, that she's nervous.

"I dunno," I say. "I guess I'll go to church and try to stay out of my mom's hair. Maybe hang with Foxxy. You know, Sunday."

As Erica is looking through more backdrops she asks, "Would you like to have dinner at my house Sunday night?"

Wow. I mean, wow! That would be great, right?

"Sure," I say. "That would be great."

"Oh, here's a backdrop that might go perfectly," she says. "What do you think of this?"

It's okay. I mean, everything is okay. I'm having dinner with Erica on Sunday night.

"I think it's perfect," I tell her.

And it's true. It's all perfect. Am I on a roll or what?

DUKE

I'm too busy to share deep thoughts about my life, so instead I will resort, for the moment at least, to the epistolary[15] form. I'm not going to use letters as much as terse entries of thoughts, as if in a diary. Apologies, dear reader, but as you will soon learn, I am tremendously busy and time is short.

....
15. Of or associated with letters or the writing of letters.

Monday

Note from Sharon in my locker:

Hi Duke,
Hope you had a great weekend.
See you at student council.
                    —S

I shot right back:

Dearest,
It was a long and lonely weekend without you.
Pining for you,
DVS[16]

   Early-morning meeting with Mr. Lichtensteiner, Mr. Porter, and Miranda Mullaly. Choice between dance or NYC Nights. I begin to lobby for the dance. That afternoon, Sam Dolan gets the jerks in the student council to vote for NYC Nights. I hide my disappointment, end meeting, begin working with Mr. Porter.

....

16. Not sure if this will stick, but trying it out for now. I can't imagine signing Duke Vanderbilt Samagura endlessly when my first novel is published.

Note: Mr. Porter struggles with basic math. Not sure if we'll be able to pull this off.

I'm also a little angry with Sam.

Tuesday

Check in on spirit committee. Sharon and Ralph working on a jingle to play over morning announcements. Ralph a little too excited. Sharon appears serious and businesslike.

There are forms to fill out for the police and fire dept. I can't trust Mr. Porter to do them correctly, or even edit them. I'll have Sharon give them a once-over.

Wednesday

Jingle coming along. Sharon and Ralph Waldo perform it for me to the tune of "You're Never Fully Dressed Without a Smile":

Sharon: Hey, sixth-graders.
Ralph: Hey, seventh-graders.

Sharon: You've got your own style.

Ralph: But, brother, you're never fully dressed without a smile.

Ralph: Hey, teachers and,

Sharon: Hey, administrators

Ralph: You've got your own style.

Sharon: But, brother, you're never fully dressed without a smile.

(Piano riff here, provided by Mr. Wexler, the Judas.)

Sharon: Are you in need of a smile?

Ralph: If so, we have the cure. New York City Nights, the Penn Valley Middle School talent, comedy, dance, art extravaganza.

Sharon: We have it all. So remember . . .

Both: You're never fully dressed without a smile.

Ralph is quite proud of this work. He thought it was brilliant. I thought it was too much and missing the point. Sharon said it wasn't an advertisement for the Super Bowl. She's probably right.

Knuckles and Moose watch from across the room, ready to pounce.

Thursday

Ralph and Sharon record the duet in the music room. Mrs. Lambert accompanies them on the piano. Mr. Wexler, once my mentor, disappointed me by coaching them.

I'll hatch a plan to get back at Ralph.

Sharon is thrilled with the spirit committee's progress. I feign interest.

Busy with commencement speech. Perusing great eulogies for inspiration.

Friday

Note from Sharon in my locker first thing in the morning.

Duke,
So busy I forgot to ask. Would you like to have
dinner with my family Sunday night?
           —S

I immediately respond:

Sharon,
Your request made my day.
I'd be delighted.
Yours always,
DVS

Ralph Waldo watched me slip the note in Sharon's locker.

Ha!

6

Meet the Parents Eve
(Anticipation)

DUKE

TODAY I FINALLY have a little bit of peace, a respite from the stress of working closely with Mr. Porter. I planned to use this time to work on an act for the talent show which will show off the dancing skills of Sharon and yours truly, but my nerves are now frayed thinking about the Sunday dinner. I'm not too much of a man to admit I'm extremely distracted. So, unable to get any work done, my only choice to keep my mind occupied was to bake a pie. A little something to offer my hosts, the Dolans.

Neal and Cassandra insisted on helping, and against my better judgment, I allowed them to join me in the kitchen, provided they did not ask questions about Sharon. It wasn't too bad, looking back on it now. They chatted about their favorite subject, their next book.[17] They did not get in my way too much. But once the pie was in the oven, I had to choose: indulge their inane conversation or march upstairs to be alone with my thoughts once again. I'm sure my choice goes without saying.

The smell of the cherry pie filled the house and I decided it might be best to prepare for the evening by writing a script. And although I am not foolish enough to believe it will work out as written, it gives me a chance to practice my lines, if you will. Mostly, it gives me a rough idea of the topic of conversation, though one never knows how a dinner party's conversation will truly run its course.

SCENE ONE

LIGHTS UP

THE DINING ROOM of the Dolan residence. DUKE, fourteen, sits at the table with SHARON, MR. DOLAN, and MRS. DOLAN. They have completed dinner and are enjoying coffee and tea.

----

17. They are planning on a little pamphlet as a guide for student protesters. It was difficult for me not to stick my head in the oven along with the pie.

Duke

Dinner was a triumph, Mrs. Dolan. I don't think I've ever enjoyed better lamb chops.

Mrs. Dolan

I'm very happy you enjoyed it, Duke.

Duke

It's a pity Sam couldn't join us. Will he be in the hospital for long?

Mr. Dolan

A couple of weeks, tops. But enough of Sam. Please, tell us more about your plans for the future.

Duke

I'm planning on attending either Harvard or Princeton[18] when I graduate from high school. Right now I'm considering a double major, international relations and pre-med.

....

18. Nothing against Harvard, but I'm very much leaning toward attending Princeton. It's only an hour away from Penn Valley, where Sharon will be during my freshman year.

Mr. Dolan

Very impressive.

Mrs. Dolan

Those are difficult schools to get into.

Duke

Both Harvard and Princeton accept only the cream of the crop, as they say. And that's why I've been preparing even while in the eighth grade. I'm currently the student council president, the sports editor of the school newspaper, and the editor in chief of the yearbook committee. My grades are impeccable. And, lest we forget, I shared the stage with Sharon as the lead in this year's spring musical.

(Duke holds out his hand. Sharon takes it.)

Mr. Dolan

You certainly seem to have your wits about you.

Mrs. Dolan

Such a polite and talented young man.

(Mr. and Mrs. Dolan take each other's hands and smile happily.)

FADE TO BLACK

I felt a bit better after writing this scene. One must be prepared for anything, of course, but with a little luck, perhaps I'd be able to steer the dinner conversation my way.

SAM

I'm nervous as soon as Erica invites me over for dinner.

No, that's not true. I'm originally excited about having dinner with Erica and her family. I mean, you don't invite someone over for dinner if you don't like them, right?

Then Foxxy says something on Friday that freaks me out.

"Let me give you some advice," he says as we're walking to lunch.

"Why do I need advice from you?" I say. "You don't even have a girlfriend anymore."

Foxxy raises his eyebrows in a disapproving way, the same way Mr. Minkin does when you ask for permission to use the bathroom in class.

"Yeah," he says. "But I can still tell you what happened

when I had dinner with Holly's parents before the . . ."

"The breakup," I suggest.

"I can't say the word," Foxxy says. "Anyway, you're going to have to stay on Mr. Dickerson's good side. And don't even look at Erica's sisters, Jane and Rosie. Mr. Dickerson is very protective of his daughters. He once sent his dogs after my brother Johnny."

I instantly get an image of dogs chasing me down the street. And just like in all my worst nightmares, for some reason I'm in my underwear. I quickly change the subject.

"So what's new with Holly and Curt Goodwin?" I ask.

Foxxy stops and bends over in pain, like he's been punched in the gut.

"Ah, don't ask that, Sam. It's like a punch in the gut."

Then I see Jenny Rios (#2 on my list), and I leave Foxxy alone in his pain. The interview doesn't go very well.

Me: Hey, Jenny.

Jenny: Hi, Sam.

Me: What do you think of Foxxy?

Jenny: I don't think of Foxxy.

Me: Why not?

Jenny: I try not to think of unpleasant things like war, famine, and your pal Foxxy.

Okay, so Foxxy is not exactly a magnet attracting girls. So then why do I let what Foxxy says about dinner with Erica bother me? I don't know. But I do know this: I don't think I'm going to find him another girlfriend.

Anticipation (and worrying) keeps building the rest of the day. I'm just about ready to go out of my mind. I hit a brick wall with my sketch ideas for NYC Nites, and I can't stop thinking about the dinner. What if I have to burp? What if I chew with my mouth open? What if Erica's parents start asking me tons of questions? As you can see, there's a lot that can go wrong.

Thankfully, tonight, like most Saturday nights, is what my dad calls "date night." It's time we (just me and my dad) set apart to hang out, eat pizza, and watch a movie. The best thing is that my sisters go out with my mom, so we have the place to ourselves. Not too shabby. And it's just what the doctor ordered to deal with my nervousness about dinner with Erica and her family. I can strike up a conversation with my dad about Sunday.

But then Lutz has to go and ruin it.

"Aren't you coming with us, John?" Maureen asks.

"No, I think I'll stay home," Lutz says. And just so you understand, when he says "home," he's not talking about his home but *my* home. My mom and dad's house! I can tell from my dad's face, he wants to give Lutz the boot, but I can also see my dad's had a long week and is very tired. Me, I've got too much on my mind to let Lutz bother me. It's like when the neighbor's dog barks. There's nothing you can do about it.

Lutz sticks his head in the refrigerator and asks, "Are there any cold sodas?"

Dad looks disgusted, like he's just pulled a long strand of hair from his food. That's when it hits me. Standing right in front of me is the answer to my little problem. My dad hates Lutz, so all I have to do is watch Lutz and do the exact opposite. Erica's father will love me!

I run as fast as I can to get my notebook from my room because Lutz and my dad are pure gold together.

Here's what I get:

- Do NOT fart.
- Do NOT spread out on the couch like you own the place, forcing the real owner of the couch and house to sit in an uncomfortable chair.
- Do NOT complain about the size of the television and suggest it's time to upgrade to a flat-screen HDTV.
- Be complimentary of the pizza that you did NOT pay for.

- Do NOT yell at the owner of the house to bring you a glass of ice for your soda when the owner of the house gets up to use the bathroom.
- Be sure to allow the owner of the house to watch the movie he wants to watch. If he wants to watch *Paul Blart: Mall Cop 2*, sit back quietly and enjoy it.
- Do NOT give away the ending.

The list above is all I get because my dad fell asleep exactly seven minutes after the pizza arrived and we popped in the movie. In that short time, he was able to glare at Lutz at least six times and scarf down four slices of pepperoni pizza. Very impressive.

Guess who's ready for Sunday dinner?!

CHOLLIE

This is the best week ever. Baseball has started and things are great with me and Miranda. And, to make the awesomest week ever even more awesome, my brother Billy has returned home because the couch he was sleeping on broke, and my mom, who would never admit it, misses Billy.

Even though things are going great with Miranda, I'm still nervous about the dinner with her parents. I've never done something like this before and I'm not sure what to expect. It's kind of like being behind in the count in baseball—you're not sure what pitch you're going to get and you have to protect the plate. Coach says prepare for a fastball so if you get an off-speed pitch you can adjust, but that's easier said than done. The bottom line is, you have to be ready for anything.

But how lucky am I that Billy's home? When I tell him how nervous I am about the dinner at Miranda's house, he suggests we drive over to the batting cages.

"I don't think you want to overanalyze this," he says when we're in his car. It's really like listening to a genius when Billy talks through a problem or situation with a girl.

"But still, Sunday dinner is the real deal, you know?" Billy says. He looks at me for a long time with a big smile on his face.

I can't reply because it's not very relaxing when you're in the passenger seat and the driver is looking at you the whole time.

"Who's going to be there?" he asks.

"I don't know. I guess Miranda and her mother and father."

"How about grandparents?"

"I dunno."

"How about aunts and uncles?"

"I dunno."

"Cousins?"

Thankfully we get to the batting cages, because I'm sure Billy has more questions about who's going to be there.

"Now, judging from how Mr. Mullaly behaved when you guys shoveled his walk and destroyed his car, I'd say he is the kind of guy who likes to be in control of things."

"You think Mr. Mullaly will bring up what happened to his car?"

"If he does, I suggest you laugh it off and say it's water under the bridge."

"Water under the bridge," I repeat.

"And I think it would be wise to bring flowers for her mother. She'll love that."

"What about Miranda?"

"You give her one flower, and the rest of the bunch goes to Miranda's mom. All girls love that because they secretly love their mothers."

"I didn't know that," I say. I learn more from Billy than from all my classes combined.

"Most importantly you want to be cool with her dad. Girls adore their fathers. You stick close to him and I think you'll be just fine."

"Wow, Billy, where'd you learn all this stuff?"

"Paying attention, that's how," he says. "You just follow my advice and nothing will go wrong."

And am I ever relaxed. Having Billy back is just like having an ace up my sleeve. I can't lose.

7

Meet the Parents

DUKE

IMAGINE HOW I felt when Sam Dolan answered the door, wearing a tattered shirt and a dirty cap (inside the house!—no manners) that I was sure I would see him wearing tomorrow at school.

"What the heck are you doing here?" Sam asked.

"I'm here for dinner. I was invited by your lovely sister."

He looked at the cherry pie.

"How do you know my sisters? And what's with the pie?" he asked. (As you continue to read this narrative you may begin to think Sam is an idiot, and you would be correct.)

"It's a cherry pie. I baked it for dessert."

From out of nowhere a big, burly chap of about sixteen years walked by, grabbed the pie from my outstretched hands, and bellowed, "This is Sharon's boyfriend!"

"He's Sharon's WHAT?" Sam exclaimed, rather rudely. Really, how oblivious can one person be? I'm sure Sharon talks about me constantly, but Sam has the attention span of a gnat.

Sam continued to stand there in an apoplectic state until the fellow who took the pie returned and said, "Come on in."

I followed Sam and the fellow into the house. Sam fell into a sofa in what would best be described as a rec room, as if he'd just done an honest day's work. Next to him was, I guessed, Sharon's sister, Maureen, who is a very attractive freshman at Penn Valley High. The slovenly lad plopped down next to Maureen. He put his feet obnoxiously on the coffee table before him. A grimy toe stuck out from his right sock.

I stood at the threshold, waiting to be announced, as the three stared at some type of zombie program on the television. It was difficult to discern the difference between the walking dead on-screen and the brain-dead teenagers sprawled out like alligators in the morning sun.

I straightened my bow tie, thinking perhaps I was a bit overdressed for the occasion.

"Sharon will be downstairs in a few," Maureen said during a commercial.

No one had the common decency to offer me a seat, so I stood and watched the show for what seemed to be a very, very long time. From what I could ascertain, the zombies rather enjoy, and perhaps even need, human brains. Sam would be perfectly safe, obviously, if this were ever to become true.

At length Sharon descended the stairs and joined us. She quickly introduced me to her sister, Maureen, and Maureen's boyfriend, John Lutz, who miraculously had made it to the tenth grade.[19] When the show resumed, Sharon shielded her eyes from the rubbish spewing from the television. That's my girl!

"Come along with me," she said, and I followed her into an adjacent little sunporch. I was delighted to see books, this month's *Atlantic Monthly*, the Sunday paper, and no television.

"Do you like crosswords?" she asked.

"I don't like them," I answered. "I love them."

....

19. When I have some free time, I'm going to write an article about the grade inflation that is rampant throughout Penn Valley and, sadly, the nation.

So Sharon and I sat on the sofa and worked on the Sunday crossword together. An odd noise came from the other room. No doubt a zombie was feasting on brains.

"What is that show they're watching?" I asked.

"*The Walking Dead*," she answered.

Recalling how she covered her face when she was in the room, I asked, "You don't like it?"

"I don't like it," she said. "I love it." She looked up at me, smiling. "That's why I covered my face. I'm recording it so I can watch it later. No spoilers!"

I returned my gaze to the crossword, trying to remember the name of a tributary to the Rhine River.

"Have you seen it?" she asked.

"The zombie show?"

"Yeah."

"No, I haven't. But if you recommend it, I certainly will," I said.

How could this girl who quoted Sherlock Holmes fall for a brainless (pun intended) television program like *The Walking Dead*? I was confused. It just didn't make sense. I stared at her pretty face while she concentrated on the crossword.

"Oh, here, *Tempest* spirit," she said. "Ariel." And she wrote it in as I gawked in awe.

We had almost polished off the crossword when we were called in for dinner.

I was shocked to see everyone seated except for Mrs. Dolan, who had an apron round her waist like it was the nineteen fifties.

"May I help?" I asked Mrs. Dolan as she brought the food to the table.

"Sure, thanks," she said. "If you could please lie those peas down next to the mashed potatoes."

"Lay," I said.

"I beg your pardon?"

"The proper verb is 'lay.' Lay the peas next to the mashed potatoes," I said.

"*Lay* the peas next to the mashed potatoes," said Mrs. Dolan with a bit of asperity.

"Here, give me the stinking peas," Mr. Dolan said, and grabbed them from me.

I got the feeling my grammatical aid was not welcome here, and I quickly changed the subject.

"Where's Sam? Won't he be joining us?"

The big guy named Lutz said, "He's having dinner with his future ex-girlfriend."

Maureen laughed at this almost-clever comment. "Oh, John, you can be so funny sometimes," she said.

I quickly noticed Sharon did not think it was funny, and Mr. Dolan was not hiding the fact he did not like this interloper. I had a hopeful feeling Lutz would make my night much easier.

Mrs. Dolan sat down and Mr. Dolan led us in a quick prayer in which we expressed gratitude for the food in front of us. And then began a free-for-all. There was plenty of food and every plate was piled high with slightly overdone roast beef, carrots, mashed potatoes, peas, and bread and butter. I felt as if I were in the kitchen of a farmhouse. The food was plain, and everyone was at the table to do one thing. And it was done well. After what I would guess to be about eight minutes, and almost on cue, we slowed down, our plates half-empty, and conversation began.

"Duke, you're in the eighth grade, is that correct?" Mrs. Dolan asked.

"That is correct," I said.

"And will you be attending Penn Valley High?" she asked.

"Yes, indeed," I answered. "Rather looking forward to it."

"I'll keep an eye on you," Lutz said. "You're not planning on wearing bow ties, right?"

"I think a bow tie is very appropriate for many occasions. And I certainly expect there will be such occasions at Penn Valley High."

"You just might not want to wear a bow tie on Freshman Day," Lutz said.

"Don't worry, Duke," Maureen said as she gave herself more peas. "John will protect you. Want some more peas?" she asked him.

"Yeah, but less than you gave yourself," Lutz said.

"Actually," I felt I should interject, "it's 'fewer' and not 'less' in this instance."

I got the feeling Lutz was no longer going to protect me on this so-called Freshman Day. He gave me a dirty look and said, "Yeah, the bow tie and correcting people's grammar will go over real good in high school."

I refrained from telling Lutz that correcting people's grammar will go over really *well* in high school.

Sharon coughed politely. "Actually, Lutz is correct. You only use 'fewer' when you know the exact number of something. So unless you know the exact number of peas in the bowl or on the spoon, 'less' is correct in this case. You wouldn't say fewer rice, would you?"

I looked at Sharon, but she immediately turned away.[20] An awkward silence fell over us until Mr. Dolan spoke.

....

20. According to *The Chicago Manual of Style*, I am indeed correct in insisting on "fewer." In Sharon's defense, however, many sources promote using "less" rather than "fewer." And she makes a good point about rice.

"Hand them here," he said, and scooped the remaining peas onto his plate. "Now there are no more peas."

The rest of the evening I was a bit more subdued. Later, after I bid my dinner companions farewell, Sharon and I waited, rather romantically, on her front porch for Neal and Cassandra to pick me up.

"Did you like the pie?" I asked Sharon.

"It was very good," she said.

"Did you think the crust was dry?"

"It doesn't matter, Duke. It wasn't a contest. There wasn't another pie to compare it to, you know."

Good point, I thought, nodding.

We waited in silence until Sharon politely coughed. She often does this before she speaks, and I find it utterly charming.

"Duke, I hope I didn't embarrass you when I corrected your grammar," she said.

"No, not at all," I said. "We all make mistakes."

"Yes, that's true. So if you really think that, well, then, you should let some grammatical errors go."

"Of course," I replied. "But we can always benefit from learning something new."

She was about to say something else when Neal and Cassandra pulled up.

I took Sharon's hand.

"Good night, good night! Parting is such sweet sorrow. That I shall say good night till it be morrow."

"I think you should just say it once and call it a night," she said. She let go of my hand, adding, "Good night, Romeo."

Perfect, absolutely perfect. I don't think there is another girl at Penn Valley who would know I was quoting from *Romeo and Juliet*.

CHOLLIE

The Mullaly house certainly looks different from the last time I was there. The snow is gone and the trees have leaves again. I try to concentrate on how pretty everything looks to keep from getting nervous.

I ring the doorbell and after about ten seconds Mr. Mullaly answers. He's wearing tan pants and a blue shirt and white shoes. (I only say this because last time I saw him he was chasing me down the street in his underwear.) He's got a smile on his face.

"Hi, I'm Chollie Muller," I say, and stick out my hand. "Charlie Muller, I mean."

Mr. Mullaly gives me a good firm handshake but not

like he wants to beat me up, which I take as a positive sign.

"Chet Mullaly. Nice to meet you," he says, and steps aside to let me enter.

And it's all clear sailing from there. I meet Mrs. Mullaly and give her the flowers. I don't get a chance to take one to give to Miranda, but I think that's okay. Miranda has a big smile as she watches her mother put the flowers in a vase with water.

Then we all sit at the kitchen table and her parents drink coffee and Miranda and I have iced tea. We talk about school and NYC Nites and the baseball team. It's all so easy, and the cool thing is that her parents seem really interested in what we have to say, even though I more or less just say "yup" and "sure."

After a while Mr. Mullaly is ready to fire up the grill and asks me if I want to come along with him.

"Go ahead, Charlie," Miranda says. "We'll make the salad."

So off I go with Mr. Mullaly, and he's got some kind of awesome setup in the backyard. The grill is huge and has a built-in refrigerator next to it and even a sink.

"You like steak, Charlie?" Mr. Mullaly asks.

"Oh, you bet I do. I love steak. There's nothing like a good steak."

Mr. Mullaly opens the refrigerator and pulls out huge steaks covered in salt and pepper.

"Let's give the grill about fifteen minutes to get going, then we'll toss these bad boys on," he says as he admires the steaks.

At first I think fifteen minutes is a long time to sit around and talk. And I really don't have much to say.

"You know what's on these steaks, Charlie?"

"No, sir," I say.

"Just a little bit of olive oil, salt, and pepper. That's all a steak needs."

All I know about steaks is that I like to eat them. So I just nod and worry about what we're going to talk about next.

But did we ever have stuff to talk about! Mr. Mullaly must read the sports page from beginning to end every day. He knows everything you could ever know. And he's actually been to a bunch of amazing sports events. Can you believe that he was at the Phillies game when they won the World Series in 2008 and the Linc when the Eagles won the NFC championship in 2004? I just couldn't believe it and I kept right on asking him questions and he kept right on answering them. It's awesome to have a guy like that to talk to.

Mr. Mullaly does all this talking as he's grilling the steaks. I can hear them sizzling and the smell is just incredible. There's really nothing like it.

"Charlie, I hope you like your steak medium rare. I just can't do it any other way," Mr. Mullaly says as he takes them off the grill.

"That's fine with me, sir," I say as I watch zucchini grill right next to the steaks.

I guess he notices me watching because he explains what he's doing. "The zucchinis will pick up the flavor from the steak."

"What about those up there?" I ask.

"These," he says, pointing to the zucchinis on the top rack, "are for Miranda. She won't eat them if they touch the meat."

I'm just about to ask why when Miranda and her mother come out of the kitchen with a big, giant salad that looks like it's for a big, giant rabbit.

When we sit down, I notice there are only three steaks, and even though they're super big, I kind of feel disappointed, since I'm sure I'll have to share mine with Miranda.

Mr. Mullaly gives me a steak first.

"That's a pretty big steak. I can share mine with Miranda," I say.

All the Mullalys look at each other and smile.

"Charlie," Miranda says, "I'm a vegetarian."

"What, like an animal doctor?" I ask.

"A vegetarian. I don't eat meat."

I feel a little silly and smile. It's sort of a shame that she's missing this awesome steak. But she just takes a bunch of salad and the zucchinis that don't have any flavor from the meat.

"Looks good," Mrs. Mullaly says.

"Dig in," Mr. Mullaly says.

And that's exactly what I do.

It's the best steak I've ever had in my life. It's perfect.

"Geez, Mr. Mullaly, this is perfect," I say.

"I'm glad you like it," he says.

"I'm not kidding. You could sell this in a restaurant."

Nobody says anything for a little bit, so I use Billy's advice and ask questions.

"How long have you been a vegetarian, Miranda?" I ask.

"Two years," she says.

Billy always says to follow up a question with another question. It's the way to get conversations going, especially in a situation like a dinner party, which is sort of what tonight is.

"Why?" I ask.

"Why what?" Miranda asks.

"Why are you a vegetarian?"

"There are a thousand reasons to be a vegetarian. But

let me just give you a couple. One, I believe it's inhumane to eat another living thing. Two, it's terrible for the environment. Do you know that raising cattle contributes to global warming? The amount of food we grow to feed the cattle is enough to feed the world."

I don't know what to say. "I'm sorry."

"Charlie, it's fine. It's a personal choice. And it's great knowing that we'll be raising money at NYC Nites for the Penn Valley Vegetarian Society."

I have to say I'm pretty relieved Miranda isn't more upset about us eating steaks. I've seen her get pretty passionate at student council meetings. Still, just to be sure, I don't say anything else about the awesomeness of the steak. It's so good, I have to slow down so I'm not the first one finished. I only eat the rest of my steak when I look at Mr. Mullaly's plate and see that it's almost clean.

Mr. Mullaly helps change the subject by asking who I think the Sixers should pick in the draft.

And then it gets even better because after dinner Mrs. Mullaly says me and Mr. Mullaly could go into the living room and watch some of the basketball play-offs. So we're sitting there flipping between the basketball and baseball games, and after a while (I have no idea how long, that's how easy and natural the conversation is) Miranda brings us in a little cake with vanilla ice cream and supersweet strawberries.

I gotta say I don't think it can get any better than this.

MIRANDA

To: Erica

From: Miranda

Date: April 10, 2016 8:57 PM

Subject: Dinner Disaster

E,

How was dinner with Sam?

I'm in shock here. I really am. No joke: I'm typing this e-mail while Charlie is in the living room watching sports on TV with my dad. I mean, who's his date anyway?!

On the one hand, it's great that they're getting along. I was a bit worried since the last time my dad saw Charlie he was chasing him down the street, thinking Charlie smashed in his car window. But once Charlie and my dad got talking about sports, they didn't stop. I guess I should be happy they hit it

off? I just wish I would've had more time alone with Charlie.
We never seem to get that at school because we're both
so busy. How is this harder than dating Tom, who went to a
completely different school?

Anyway, I'm dying to hear about your dinner with Sam.

xoxo

M

SAM

I get to the Dickerson house a little bit late because after
seeing my mother make such a big deal about Duke baking
a stupid pie, I run off to the store before I go to Erica's house
for dinner. I'm kind of out of breath and starting to get really sweaty and slimy. And all because of Duke and Sharon.
Did anyone see that pair coming?

Mr. Dickerson answers the door the moment I ring
the bell.

"Hiya," I say. "I'm Sam Dolan."

"Come in," he says, staring at me. "Dolan, eh. Weren't

you involved in the snowball fight over at the Mullaly house?" he asks, sticking out his hand.

"It was all a big misunderstanding," I say.

His meaty mitt practically swallows up my hand when we shake. It's a huge hand. A hairy hand. A hand capable of breaking things. If Mr. Dickerson smashed a concrete block with his fist, no one would cheer. It would be expected. The concrete block wouldn't stand a chance. Am I making myself clear? So between that hand and the way he snarls at me, I'm not feeling very confident about being in the Dickerson household.

"Here's some flowers," I say, and hand them to him.

Mr. Dickerson gives the flowers a dirty look, as if the flowers said something rude to him. It's a little weird.

Then Mr. Dickerson looks at me the way Lichtensteiner does, but even meaner. It's how Lichtensteiner would look at me if I was going out with his daughter instead of simply going to his school.

"They're for Mrs. Dickerson," I explain.

"She's allergic to flowers," he says.

"Every kind of flower?" I ask.

I get the feeling Mr. Dickerson doesn't like getting asked a lot of questions. Fortunately, at that moment, Mrs. Dickerson enters . . . and sneezes. Great.

"Hello, Sam," she says as we shake hands.

We all stand there and we don't say anything except for "God bless you" when Mrs. Dickerson sneezes again.

Then Erica enters the living room.

"Hey, Sam."

"Hi, Erica," I say.

"Dinner's almost ready," Mrs. Dickerson says. "I hope you're hungry, Sam."

"You bet," I say.

Erica catches me up on the latest Foxxy-Holly drama because now she's Foxxy's therapist. I try my best to sound interested, but I'm just so sick of hearing about Foxxy, I really am. And I'm sort of sweating a lot because I'm still nervous.

Thankfully, there isn't a long wait for dinner, since I got there a little late because I had to get the apparently poisonous flowers.

We sit down and the food looks great.

First thing I notice is that Foxxy is an idiot. Erica's sisters are pretty, but they're nothing compared to Erica. Rosie has blonde hair, and Jane has black hair, but there's just something about Erica.

And even better than sitting at the table with my gorgeous girlfriend is the salmon.

I mean, I never had anything like this before. The salmon is perfect and there's a sweet green sauce on top and the potatoes taste great and the asparagus is perfectly cooked.

"Wow, Mrs. Dickerson, this is super awesome," I say when I'm about halfway done. "My mom likes to overcook everything, but this is just right."

"Oh, but you should be complimenting my husband. I'm just the sous chef."

"Oh, geez, I'm sorry. This is awesome, Mr. Dickerson," I say.

"Glad you like it, Sam," he says. "And Mr. Dickerson is my dad. Call me Eric."

"Okay."

"Would you like some more?" he asks.

"Sure." And after Mr. Dickerson gives me some more fish I say, "Thanks, Erica."

Mr. Dickerson, I get the feeling, does not like to be called Erica.

"Eric, I mean," I mumble. "Thanks, Eric."

I decide I shouldn't do any more talking, so I go back to my fish and keep my head down.

When I look up from my plate, everyone is staring at me.

"So how'd you do it?" I break the silence.

"Do you cook?" he asks.

"Never. In my house my mom won't even let me in the kitchen," I say.

Mr. Dickerson gives me a look like he's offended, as if I've said something wrong. He gets up and starts clearing the table.

"Thanks, Erica," I say when he takes my plate. "I mean, Eric. Mr. Eric. Mr. Dickerson."

Mrs. Dickerson sneezes and Mr. Dickerson looks at the flowers.

"That's enough of these flowers," he says. He grabs the vase in his giant hand and walks to the back door. He opens the door and tosses out the flowers. The dogs growl.

When he returns, Mr. Dickerson looks me right in the eye. For some reason I think he wishes he could've thrown me out the back door with the flowers. He smiles and I think he's smiling because he's thinking of the sound of his dogs tearing my flesh from my bones.

"Thank you, Mr. Eric and Mrs. Dickerson, for a wonderful dinner," I say.

"We're glad you enjoyed it, Sam," Mrs. Dickerson says.

Mr. Dickerson gives me a quick nod. It's not much, but I'll take it.

Then Erica grabs my hand and pulls me from the table.

"Let's go," she says, and we rush out of the kitchen. I can hear Rosie and Jane giggling as we leave.

Erica leads me to the basement, which is a really big room with huge, long, and supersoft couches. Nailed to the wall is the largest big-screen television I've ever seen in my life.

"Geez, that's a big television. I'd love to watch an HBO comedy special here," I say.

"Stay on my dad's good side and maybe you can."

"Stay on his good side?" I say. "I don't think he likes me at all."

Erica grabs the remote and turns on the television.

"Is your father always this uptight?" I ask.

"You actually caught him in a good mood."

We sit on the couch and I'm practically swimming in cushions.

"Guess what we're going to watch?" she asks with a huge smile on her face. I'm not sure what's going on, but I know enough that I better smile back.

The movie starts and the music sounds a little familiar, but I'm not sure what it is. I can tell it's pretty old, even though it's in color.

"You know it yet?" Erica asks.

"Not yet," I say.

I watch this dude walk into a factory and lots of music is playing and there's a bunch of girls working on sewing machines and then it hits me.

"*The Pajama Game*!"

"That's right. Our special musical, and now our special movie."

Before break, I was twirling Erica on a stage like that. We danced a tango like nobody's business.

Erica holds my hand and sits back with that huge smile on her face.

They all start singing and dancing in the movie and it's pretty neat, especially since I know all the songs and moves.

Then Erica cuddles up close to me and something terrible happens. I feel like I have to fart. I mean, I really have to release some gas. It's probably not good for me to hold it in. My God, what am I going to do?!

And I can't cuddle up with Erica, knowing her father is upstairs. I can hear his footsteps. It sounds like there's a tiger pacing in a cage above us. What's he doing up there?

So we go on watching and I'm in pain, real serious pain, trying to hold everything in. And I guess it doesn't help that I can hear Mr. Dickerson's footsteps above and the sound of the back door opening and those dogs coming in.

When the movie is about halfway over (the part when Babe gets fired for messing up the sewing machine, if you're interested), Rosie and Jane call down.

"Sam and Erica, break it up," they say.

Erica gives me her great smile.

"Sam, we're ready to drive you home," Rosie or Jane says.

I get in the back of the car with Rosie and Erica as Jane drives. Mr. Dickerson chews on an unlit cigar and sits in the passenger seat. He sits sideways so he can watch Jane practice driving, but I get the feeling he's staring at me.

All I can think about is the fart. I mean, could you imagine if I let loose in the car on a chilly night with the windows up?

Thankfully, I get home. I'm so happy to be in the fresh, open night air that I don't even mind seeing Duke holding Sharon's hand.

I mean, I've never been happier to be home.

ERICA

To: Miranda

From: Erica

Date: April 10, 2016 9:07 PM

Subject: Dinner Disaster

M,

What is *wrong* with boys? Your boyfriend would rather be on a date with your dad and mine wanted nothing to do with me! Dinner went as good as can be expected (you know my dad, always the tough guy). But when I invited Sam to watch *The Pajama Game* (romantic, right?!), it seemed like he kept trying to move away from me. I'd get close to hold his hand and he'd pull away. At one point, I swear he tried to use the sofa cushions as some kind of fort between us. He had a stupid look on his face the whole time, too—like he was trying to hold in a fart or something. What a weirdo. I think I'll ask Foxxy if he knows what Sam's problem is. . . .

E

8

Freewriting

Duke Vanderbilt Samagura

21 April 2016

English 8A

Mr. Minkin

Suggested Writing Prompt: *If you could change yourself in three ways, what would they be? How would these changes affect your past, your present, and your future? Explain.*

Sir:

Unlike you, who refuse to change your mediocre teaching ways and follow the simplest advice I have graciously offered, I am not beyond self-criticism as a means of self-improvement. Let's make a list, shall we?

- I would change my appearance and be a bit more physically imposing. More like my good friends Knuckles and Moose, I suppose.
- I would change my name.
- I would change my personality, just a bit, and be a little less—just a little bit less, mind you— critical of my peers and adults.

I think if I was a little less critical of my peers and adults, dinner with the Dolans would have gone a bit better. I was not on my best behavior on Sunday. Perhaps I was simply nervous. After all, it was the first time I was meeting Sharon's parents. Or maybe I'm simply wound a little too tight. Who could blame me after the years of negligence and downright poor parenting from Neal and Cassandra?

At any rate, Sharon is correct in her claim that I may have been a tad rude.

I shouldn't have corrected her mother for using "lie" when she should have said "lay."

And I shouldn't have corrected her sister's

boyfriend for saying "less" when he should have said "fewer."

I will, however, stand by my telling Maureen's boyfriend that it is bloody bad form to belch at the dinner table.

Still, I should make these changes because, as Sharon so perfectly pointed out, not everyone is like me. And not everyone is interested in using proper grammar every moment of the day. Sharon certainly knows how to use "lay" and "lie" properly, yet at the same time she very much enjoys her family patois.

I'm actually looking forward to loosening up a little bit. It will certainly help my writing, especially my plays and screenplays. Capturing the language of the common man is essential for capturing the verisimilitude (to save you some time, Mr. Minkin, "verisimilitude" means truth) of life that is essential in all great works of literature.

And now that I think about it, perhaps the ability to partake in some friendly conversation will help when I interview with the admissions officers at Princeton and Harvard.

Sam Dolan

April 21st 2016

English 8A

Mr. Minkin

Suggested Writing Prompt: *If you could change yourself in three ways, what would they be? How would these changes affect your past, your present, and your future? Explain.*

Hey Mr. Minkin,

Great question! I don't know if I can think of three things to change about myself, but I would definitely change one.

If I could I would procrastinate much less. I swear I've been going home right after school every day to work on my portion of NYC Nites. But you'll never believe what's been happening. I get nothing, absolutely nothing, done. And boy does the time ever fly. The fastest two hours in history are those two hours that I sit at my desk to make a list of people I should try to book for the talent show. Before I know it it's time for dinner and I have a whole lot of nothing.

Like yesterday I got home and I had an idea for a skit about what happened last year on the seventh-grade class trip at the zoo. I'm sure you heard a version of what happened, but this is the truth:

If you remember, every kid in the Philadelphia area was at the zoo that day. And when me and Foxxy were checking out the monkeys, some kids climbed up on the fence. That caused an alarm to go off and Foxxy started running. Of course I started running with Foxxy because when you see somebody running and he's your best friend, you just run along with him. Next thing you know there's a bunch of security guards chasing us through the zoo and Foxxy kept on going so I kept on going too.

I thought they had those tranquilizer guns in case an animal gets out.

Of course, when they got us to the security office, that's when they looked at the surveillance and saw that it wasn't me and it wasn't Foxxy. But it didn't matter at that point. Me and Foxxy were out cold from the tranquilizers.

But geez, how do you write something like that and make it funny?

And, oh yeah, it would also be nice if I didn't have to go to the bathroom after every meal. That really ruined dinner at Erica's house. I'd like to make that little change too.

Chollie Muller

April 21, 2016

English 8A

Mr. Minkin

Suggested Writing Prompt: *If you could change yourself in three ways, what would they be? How would these changes affect your past, your present, and your future? Explain.*

Dear Mr. Minkin,

You probably get a lot of really good answers to this question. But I have to tell you, my brother Billy wouldn't like it at all. My mom is always trying to get him to change. Mostly things like waking up earlier in the morning and cleaning up after himself. He also gets a lot of parking tickets, doesn't really have a place to live, and works as a pizza delivery guy.

Billy always argues that we shouldn't change. And he's a real good arguer. He'll say if he makes all these big changes he won't be Billy anymore but some stranger who cleans up after himself and wakes up early and doesn't get parking tickets. And then Billy turns it all around on my mom and makes my mom feel bad.

Okay, I know it looks like I've been stalling to answer the question. I guess it's because I'm not sure if Billy's right about not changing. Sometimes I wonder if Miranda wants me to be more like her ex-boyfriend, this guy named Tom Nelson who goes to another school. She brings him up a lot and sometimes it makes me feel crummy.

At least Miranda's dad is awesome. I bet he wouldn't want me to change.

Miranda Mullaly

April 21, 2016

English 8A

Mr. Minkin

Suggested Writing Prompt: *If you could change yourself in three ways, what would they be? How would these changes affect your past, your present, and your future? Explain.*

When I'm with Charlie I often think I should change myself and try to be more relaxed. Charlie has such a wonderful way of seeing the world. He's always optimistic and believes with certainty that things will work out at the end.

Isn't that wonderful? I hope he never changes.

I, on the other hand, tend to look at the glass as half empty. And often I analyze a simple problem to the point where my solutions need solutions. But since I've begun to simplify my thinking, I've actually seen changes.

Here's a perfect example. Last year, last month in fact, if I had been told we weren't going to have a class trip I would've spent more time and energy making complaints to the school board, the principal, and the PTA. And guess what? It wouldn't have made a difference.

But now that Charlie is in my life and now that I'm viewing the world with a glass-half-full outlook, when we were told we wouldn't have a class trip I simply suggested an alternative. If we can't go to New York, we'll bring New York to us. Glass half full!

Erica Dickerson

April 21, 2016

English 8A

Mr. Minkin

Suggested Writing Prompt: *If you could change yourself in three ways, what would they be? How would these changes affect your past, your present, and your future? Explain.*

This is a really odd question to ask teenagers, Mr. Minkin. Don't you know us well enough to know that we're always thinking about making changes to ourselves? I bet if you asked every girl with brown hair what color she'd like her hair to be, she would say blonde. And every blue-eyed girl would say she wants brown eyes.

But, since you asked the question, here's my answer:

I really would change the way I look so I could be as pretty as Rosie or Jane. Yes, I'd like to have Rosie's blonde hair or Jane's curly hair, anything but my straight brown hair. So there are two changes, right there.

And these changes would definitely have an

effect on me. I'd be irresistible, like Jane and Rosie. I wouldn't be Erica, the girl next door that all the guys treat like their funny friend. Maybe then Sam would really notice me and want to <u>be</u> with me (you know, hold my hand or kiss me) instead of just <u>hang</u> with me. There is a difference.

9

The Best Laid Plans

SAM

I'M NOT LYING when I say I've been waiting to see *Joe Klipspringer and the Lady Trailblazers* since I first saw the trailer last year. This was before Foxxy and Holly Culver started going out and Foxxy and I went to watch a movie and we saw the trailer for this one. I don't want to sound like I'm crazy or anything, but if a movie preview can change your life, this one can. Foxxy and I laughed so hard during the two-minute trailer we were practically on the floor. And now there are thirty-second commercials for it on TV and they crack me up every time.

What is really awesome is that I just know Erica is going to love it. It's totally her type of humor. Really solid jokes and good physical comedy. And even though Rotten Tomatoes isn't giving it a good score, I'm certain we're going to love it.

But the crazy thing is, even though I know she's going to love it, I'm nervous about asking her. Isn't that weird? Things are just a touch off since I had dinner at her house. I'm not sure if it's because I grossed her out or if her dad said something. I just don't know.

So on Monday I really want to ask her out. But of course I'm hardly ever alone with her and when we are I get too nervous to ask her.

I have no choice but to ask Foxxy about it. I guess that's the only upside of his new friendship with Erica.

"Is Erica mad at me?" I ask.

"Nope," he says. "Everything's okey dokey."

Crap. That's the last thing I want to hear. Foxxy says things like "okey dokey" before he fails a test. And he said things were "okey dokey" with Holly Culver while Holly Culver was saying she never wanted to see him again.

Since Erica is so busy at school, and since Foxxy is always with us, I have to ask her to the movie by calling her. If I had a cell phone like a normal kid, I could text her, but God forbid my mother return it, even though I haven't been in trouble all year.

Here's the conversation when I ask my mother for my cell phone back:

Me: Hey, Mom, can I get my cell phone back?

Mom: No.

Me: But I haven't been in trouble since you took it away.

Mom: No.

Me: It's not fair.

Mom: No.

Me: What if there's an emergency?

Mom: No.

Me: What's for dinner?

Mom: No.

So that's my life. I feel just like one of the dork kids from *The Goldbergs* when I finally call Erica after dinner. We don't even have a cordless phone, so I have to drag the stupid thing from the hall into my room.

I sit on the floor, and I have an index card with some stuff I want to say.

Okay, not hard, right? I take a deep breath.

"Hello, Erica," I say when the phone is picked up.

"Is this Dolan?" It's Mr. Dickerson.

As soon as he says "Dolan," I hear the dogs growling. What's with those beasts?

"Yeah," I say. "I mean, yes, sir. I thought this was Erica's phone."

"It is," he says. "What do you want?"

"I'd like to speak to Erica, if she's not busy."

"Just a minute."

It sounds like the phone drops.

"Hello."

"Oh, Erica, thank God it's you. How are you?"

"I'm fine. Why?"

"No reason. Just being polite. Small talk, you know."

"Okay . . ." she says.

"Listen, Erica," I say, jumping right in. "Do you want to see *Joe Klipspringer and the Lady Trailblazers* with me Saturday night?"

"Sure," she says. "Sounds like fun."

"Oh, it's going to be awesome. I mean, the trailer is just about the funniest thing I've ever seen. Have you seen the commercials?"

"Is that the one about the guy who wants to play girls' basketball?"

"Exactly," I say. "That's the one. It's supposed to be hilarious."

"Uh-huh," she says, and I can tell she's not convinced

it's going to be funny. "Why does he want to play girls' basketball?"

"I guess we'll find out," I say.

Then there is an awkward pause.

"Are you still there?" Erica asks.

"Oh, yeah, okay, so we're on, you and me, for *Joe Klipspringer and the Lady Trailblazers* this weekend."

"Great," says Erica. "And I'll see if Miranda and Chollie would like to join us."

"Oh, sure," I say. There's another pause. "So I'll see you tomorrow at school."

"You sure will."

I look down at my index cards. "So," I say, "what did you have for dinner tonight?" Agh, what a stupid question. Then I hear her phone click.

"What?"

"Oh, nothing," I say.

"That's Foxxy, Sam," she says. "I gotta go."

"Oh."

DUKE

The French auteurs[21] are among my favorites artists. They

----

21. The well-deserved nomenclature used to describe French film directors. The average Hollywood hack deserves no such accolades.

know how to make a film. They know how to move a camera, how to tell a story, how to meld music perfectly with a scene. One of my favorites is *Les Parapluies de Cherbourg*,[22] so when I read a review comparing Jean des Garrenes's debut film, *La Saison des Jonquilles*, to Jacques Demy's classic, I looked immediately for when it was premiering in Penn Valley, if it was to play here at all.

So you can imagine how I felt when I read in the Sunday paper that it would indeed be playing in my hometown. I immediately resolved to take Sharon to the film this weekend. I doubt it will be playing past that, for the brain-dead denizens of Penn Valley are not known to support the arts.

Over Sunday dinner, as Neal and Cassandra droned on about troubles in the Middle East, I thought of the weekend to come. It struck me over dessert that it might be fun to build a little suspense before I asked her. So after dinner I devised a plan that would be both intriguing and mysterious. Sharon would have a blast trying to figure out what was to be.

After our tea I sat and began to work on how to make the night special. *La Saison des Jonquilles* translates to *The Season of the Daffodils*. So of course I should start off with

....

22. *The Umbrellas of Cherbourg* in English. Jacques Demy's 1964 film that inspired future generations and is considered a classic.

a note quoting a famous poem about daffodils. And where better to begin than with William Wordsworth.

> *Sharon,*
> *"For oft, when on my couch I lie*
> *In vacant or in pensive mood,*
> *They flash upon that inward eye*
> *Which is the bliss of solitude;*
> *And then my heart with pleasure fills*
> *And dances with the daffodils."*
> *William Wordsworth*
> *Looking forward to the weekend!!*
> *DVS*

After I wrote the above, I felt satisfied. And though I didn't know exactly what was next, I was confident I would come up with something. After all, I spent most of the time deciding on how many exclamation points to use. Wordsworth just popped into my head.

But the best laid plans often go awry, and Sharon, who would come across the note in the morning, was rather confused by the missive. We spoke about it after school.

"I don't understand the note," she said.

"It's the final stanza of William Wordsworth's 'I Wandered Lonely as a Cloud,'" I informed her.

"Yes, I can see that. But I don't understand what it has to do with the weekend," she said.

I panicked. I thought maybe she might have plans for the weekend. And no doubt that snake in the grass Ralph Waldo was up to no good. So I scrapped my plans for a pseudo courtship for the movie and came right out and asked her.

"The note was just my way of asking you to see *La Saison des Jonquilles* with me this weekend."

"What is *La Saison* whatever-it's-called?"

I fought off the urge to cringe. "*La Saison des Jonquilles* is a debut film from a promising French director. It won accolades at the Toronto Film Festival."

"But Toronto is in Canada," she said. I wasn't sure if she was trying to be funny. Although Sharon is a tremendous dramatic actor, she is lacking, for the present, the necessary skills in the field of humor.

"And besides," she added, "I was hoping to see *Joe Klipspringer and the Lady Trailblazers*. I'm sure it hasn't won any prizes, but it looks pretty funny."

"*La Saison des Jonquilles* might not play past this weekend," I said.

"In that case," Sharon said, "we'd better run off and see it immediately."

I laughed and we went our separate ways. I was a bit

disappointed my lavish plan did not come to full fruition. But, guess what? It worked. *La Saison des Jonquilles*, here we come!

CHOLLIE

"I don't like it," Billy says when I tell him about the plan for Saturday night.

"Why not?" I ask him.

Billy scratches his chin. "I can't help but wonder why she wants to go on a double date. I mean, it's like hanging out in a group. You're all just buddies and it gets all mixed up. Before you know it, your lady is sitting and chatting with her friend and you're sitting beside the other dude, holding hands and sharing popcorn, while Miranda is sharing Milk Duds with her best pal. Next thing you know, she's thinking, 'Who needs Chollie Muller?'"

This hits me right in the gut. It knocks the wind out of me.

When Miranda asked me to go to the movies with her and Erica and Sam, I felt great. It's perfect, I thought, double-dating at the movies. I don't want to sound corny, but it just seemed really grown-up and mature and super fun. It sort of seemed like the thing Billy would do, if he had a girlfriend.

But now Billy's got me worried about it. Now I'm wishing I was going over to Miranda's house and chilling and watching basketball with her dad instead of going to the movies.

"What am I going to do now, Billy?"

"Fortunately, there are a couple of things we can do to solve the problem. When you get to the theater, suggest you two, just you and Miranda, go to another movie. What's the plan now?"

I have it all written down in my notebook.

"We're going to see *Joe Klipspringer and the Lady Trailblazers* at seven."

"Where?"

"The AMC at the mall."

"Okay," Billy says. "Let's see what else we have going on at that AMC."

Billy looks on his phone and reads the theater schedule.

"Oh, here it is. Perfect." Billy looks at me with a big smile.

"What is it?"

"Check this out," Billy says. "*La Saison des Jonquilles* at seven fifty-five. The unforgettable story of two best friends growing up in southern France during the turbulent sixties. It's even in French with English subtitles."

"Do you think she'll like the movie?"

"Film," Billy says. "Film. *Klipspringer* is a movie. But *La Saison des Jonquilles* is a film. And of course she'll like it. If Miranda is the girl I think she is, she'll fall in love all over again."

"Perfect. What a plan! Thanks, Billy."

"One more thing," Billy says as I'm walking out the door. "Try to stay awake. Films tend to be more boring than movies."

10

Date Night

CHOLLIE

SAM AND I GET to the movie theater at the same time Miranda and Erica get there. Miranda really looks terrific. She's wearing a purple sweater and faded jeans and brown shoes, and her hair is pulled back, so you can see her entire beautiful face. She looks so pretty I could just stare at her for the next two hours instead of going to the movie, but of course it's rude to stare. And it's also really difficult to think of things to say, which is the hardest part of a relationship. Even Billy thinks it's the most difficult part. But the good thing about seeing a movie is that you can talk about that after you see it.

"Hi, Miranda," I say.

"Hello, Charlie," she says.

I wave Miranda a little closer to me and away from Erica and Sam and whisper, "I was thinking maybe you'd like to see *La Saison des Jonquilles*. Should I get two tickets for that?"

"But we said we'd see *Joe Klipspringer and the Lady Trailblazers* with Erica and Sam," Miranda says.

"I know, but I have a good feeling about *La Saison des Jonquilles*." (Billy helped me practice saying this like a real French dude.) "It's the story of three friends growing up in the south of France during the turbulent sixties. And also," I add, "it's got French people speaking in French."

"Charlie, what's the big deal about people speaking French?" she asks.

"Don't you want to see a revelation in filmmaking?"

I point to the movie poster. It sure makes France look like a beautiful country.

And then I see the poster of *Joe Klipspringer and the Lady Trailblazers*. It's got a picture of a guy in a basketball uniform and a sweatband holding a basketball, and his teammates, the Lady Trailblazers (who are all girls), are behind him. It actually seems kind of funny.

I really don't know what to say about *Klipspringer*, but when I look at Miranda, she's smiling at the picture and so am I. It's a no-brainer. And I'm sure when I tell

Billy, he'll understand. His rule is "the lady is always right."

That smile of Miranda's just does something for me. It makes me so happy. So when Miranda sees Duke and Sharon, I don't even mind that she invites them to watch the movie with us.

And when we all sit down and I find myself next to the aisle, I don't care. When I look over at Miranda, she grins and I know she is having a good time.

Even when I burn myself on the pizza afterward, even though it hurts so much I almost cry, it's okay because Miranda gets some ice and helps with the burn.

The cherry on top is Mr. Mullaly offering to give me a ride home. He catches me up on all the basketball play-offs scores and says he is going to cut out of work early to see one of my baseball games.

What a night. Even Billy thinks it was a home run.

DUKE

Much to my chagrin, Neal and Cassandra were very excited to give Sharon and me a ride to the movie theater. Penn Valley is a typical soulless suburb, and that means we have inadequate public transportation. Therefore, I was at the mercy of my parents, though I made them swear they wouldn't talk.

Neal and Cassandra introduced themselves to Sharon and her parents, who were quite obviously thrilled to see their youngest daughter on a date with a chap like me.

Once we were all in the car, I immediately steered the conversation to Sharon and me. I didn't want Sharon to find out, at least so soon, how weird my parents are.

"That's a lovely dress," I said. "It practically matches my bow tie."

"Thank you," Sharon replied.

"Did you have a nice day at school?" I asked.

"It was okay. And you?"

"Rather tedious, I'm afraid. Most of the subject matter covered in class I have already mastered. I'm sure you feel the same way."

"Well, actually, I really enjoyed the conversation in English class. We had quite a discussion of *The Giver*. Mrs. Mikulski positively loves the book and her energy is infectious. The whole class was involved. She's a great teacher."

I scoffed. "I had Mrs. Mikulski last year. I would say she's an average teacher at best. She barely challenged us. And *The Giver*," I added, shaking my head sadly, "is hardly great literature."

Sharon was silent, most certainly contemplating whether or not Mrs. Mikulski was a good teacher. We drove the rest of the way without speaking until we pulled into the parking lot.

"Ah, *La Saison des Jonquilles*, here we come," I said with great aplomb.

And then I don't know what happened. We ran into Miranda Mullaly and Erica Dickerson, and they started talking to Sharon. The three have become rather chummy, working together on NYC Nights. The next thing I knew, I was buying tickets for *Joe Klipspringer and the Lady Trailblazers*.

In the theater I found myself stuck between Sam Dolan and Chollie Muller, both munching so loudly on the popcorn that for a minute I thought it was part of the film, or more accurately, movie. Sharon was trapped between Miranda and Erica, and when I looked over toward her, she put on a brave face, smiling and waving to me. But of course she was heartbroken, so far away from me.

Without earplugs to block out the sound of Sam laughing and Chollie chewing, I had no choice but to try to make some sense of the movie. From what I could make out, it seemed as if the protagonist, a ne'er-do-well named, you guessed it, Joe Klipspringer, sues his college, the fictional (one hopes!) Eastern Pennsylvania University (I weep for our poor Commonwealth[23]) to play on the women's basket-ball team. The university decides to allow the young man to play, figuring they would lose the lawsuit and they'll be able to make Klipspringer academically ineligible. Hilarity ensues, but someone forgot to tell the actors, the director, and the writer(s). The jokes are stale and predictable and there is hardly anything funny about disrupting the pro-ceedings of a university. What kind of a person writes this tripe?

The only saving grace of the movie is that it came to an end quickly. I looked over at Sharon and she was actually clapping and smiling as the credits rolled and they showed outtakes.

"Okay, let's go," I said to Chollie, who was blocking our exit to the aisle.

"Hang on, Duke. I heard these outtakes are brilliant," Sam said.

So I had to watch three minutes of Klipspringer miss-ing layups, falling down stairs, riding through a campus on a bicycle resembling a candy cane, and generally disgrac-ing higher education.

---

23. Pennsylvania is not a state but a commonwealth, like Massachusetts and Virginia.

"Oh, wow, look at that, Eric Heimberger was the key grip," I said sarcastically. "I didn't know Coventry Catering took care of food services. And Robin Lencheski was the scouting director. She did a great job."

"If you didn't like the movie, Duke," Sam said, "then something is wrong with you. That's the best movie you'll see all year."

I argued for coffee after we left the theater, but Chollie and Sam had their hearts set on pizza. Sharon, who in all fairness was probably excited to be out not only with me but also Erica and Miranda, wanted to join them for pizza. After all, it's only natural for a seventh-grader to look up to the eighth-graders. So my pleas to go to the coffee shop fell on deaf ears, and we took a large table at Lorenzo's.

Chollie and Sam ordered two pizzas, and I directed the conversation to the film, I mean movie. Though there was little to actually discuss, I thought it was at least of some interest that a man would play women's basketball. In fact, perhaps the only redeeming quality of the movie is that the women on the basketball team were serious about their academic endeavors.

"So," I said. "What did we think about the movie?"

"I loved it," Sam said eagerly. "I thought it was the best ever."

"Yes, I'm sure you did," I replied. "I found it profound that the protagonist couldn't pay his tuition without getting that scholarship. It also gave a very realistic, and sad, portrayal of how a person, no matter how stupid, how daft, how incorrigible, can still get his or her five minutes of fame. As a society, we seem to be drawn to people like this character Klipspringer, who is really nothing more than an idiot. The epitome of someone taking up space at college."

I looked at Miranda, who seemed dumbfounded. I can't believe I once had a crush on her.

Erica, well, she's going out with Sam Dolan. What else is there to say?

Chollie was watching the kitchen make the pizzas and probably didn't hear what I said.

Sam was fidgeting, looking like he needed to use the bathroom.

Then I looked to Sharon. It was obvious she had absorbed and contemplated what I said. She took a deep breath and jumped in.

"I don't think it really needs that type of analysis. It was fun. It was harmless. We laughed and had a good time. Can't we just leave it at that?"

I quickly changed the subject.

"So," I said, "what's your favorite Sherlock Holmes story?"

Sharon looked at me oddly. "I've never read a Sherlock Holmes story."

"But remember when you quoted Sherlock Holmes? You said you see and you observe."

Sharon laughed. "I thought I was quoting you because you were always saying it during rehearsals."

I was too shocked to reply. Fortunately, the pizzas arrived and the conversation turned to the burn Chollie sustained from the cheese.

SAM

I've never been on a double date before, so this is all really new and it's like I'm seeing the movie theater for the first time. It sounds crazy, but I've never noticed how clean the theater is, or how much it smells like buttered popcorn. Or even how the workers have real uniforms. But I notice tonight because we're on a date, a real, serious date. The guy who takes our tickets actually calls me "sir."

I must be growing up or something because even when Sharon and Duke (can you believe those two are still going out?) decide to watch *Klipspringer* with us, I don't care. I'm just not going to let anything get in the way of a terrific night with Erica.

We choose our seats and I jump over Chollie and Duke

so I can sit next to Erica. As soon as the movie starts, we (Erica and me) laugh from the beginning to the end. It might be the best movie ever made, I mean, it's that good. I'm even thinking of going to college, that's how much the movie may have changed my life.

I'm still laughing when they're showing the outtakes. I mean, I just can't take my eyes off it. Everyone's talking about what to do after, which makes me happy because now that the movie is over, I'm happy to get rid of Sharon and Duke. You can't be very romantic with your little sister tagging along.

I'm still smiling when the lights come back on. "Why don't we all go out for pizza?" Erica says.

Then Sharon says, "That's a great idea."

We all get up to go, and guess who we run into in the lobby? Foxxy. By himself. Who goes to the movies alone? I want to ask.

Before I know what's happening, Foxxy and Sharon and Duke decide to join us for pizza. All I want to do is hold Erica's hand and just be alone and this is what happens. So there I am sitting at a table for five with seven squeezed in. It's no surprise I spill soda *and* pizza on myself. It's the only nice shirt I own, and now it's going to have stains on it like all my other clothes.

Everyone at the table is suddenly an expert on getting

out stains. Foxxy jumps up to join me in the bathroom, but I glare at him and tell him to sit down.

As I'm washing out my shirt, I hear the toilet flush and who of all people comes out but Mr. Lichtensteiner. Of all the pizza joints in all the malls in all the world, why does he have to choose Lorenzo's?

"Hey, Dolan," he says.

"What are you doing here?" I ask. And I really mean it, especially since he's always asking me what I'm doing when we're in school.

"Dinner and a movie with Mrs. Lichtensteiner," he says as he washes his hands. "We saw some French movie, though I wanted to see *Klipspringer.*"

Lichtensteiner looks at my shirt.

"Did you get any pizza in your mouth, Dolan?"

Lichtensteiner leaves, and my shirt is soaking wet. I wait for a second, figuring Lutz has got to be coming next because that's what kind of night it is, but he doesn't, so I return to the table.

Now I realize I have a clear view of Lichtensteiner, who is eating like a total pig but doesn't get any food on his shirt. And Foxxy doesn't either, for once. Life sure is unfair sometimes.

When we finish up our pizza, all the couples go their

separate ways. In case you're wondering, Foxxy stays with Erica and me. We (the three of us) wait for Mr. Dickerson to pick her up. Erica offers to give me and Foxxy a ride home.

"No," I say, "we'll walk."

I wave good-bye to Erica when she gets in the car.

"Blow her a kiss," Foxxy says.

"What?"

"Blow her a kiss," he says again. "What kind of boyfriend are you anyway?"

I'm thinking of telling Foxxy I'm the kind of boyfriend who never gets a moment alone with his girlfriend, but I don't.

"Go on. Now!" Foxxy urges me.

So I blow Erica a kiss.

The only problem is that Erica turns away at that exact moment. The exact moment, by the way, that Mr. Dickerson looks at me.

ERICA

To: Miranda

From: Erica

Date: April 30, 2016 10:22 PM

Subject: What just happened?

M,

Well that was interesting, right?! See what I mean about Sam acting weird? Did you notice that he wouldn't even hold my hand? I really don't know if it's working out with him . . .

At least the movie was hilarious. Doesn't college seem like fun?

I'm glad Sharon and Foxxy could join us. They almost distracted me from how bad this date went. What Sharon sees in Duke, though, I'll never know.

Up for the mall tomorrow?

E

MIRANDA

To: Erica

From: Miranda

Date: April 30, 2016 10:27 PM

Subject: What just happened?

E,

Sam, weird? Sorry I didn't notice because Charlie didn't seem like himself. I'm not sure why he wanted to go see the French movie. Now that was weird. Why didn't he sit next to me?

And did you ever see anyone burn himself with pizza? Do you think he orders meat lovers pizza on purpose? For all the bad things about Tom, at least he always made an effort to respect my choices.

Anyway, isn't Sharon nice? I don't know what she sees in Duke but my grandmother says there's a lid for every pot. From what she told me when Duke wasn't hovering, though, she isn't so sure Duke is her lid. She said she used to find his personality a fun challenge, but now it's just exhausting. Can you blame her?

Mall tomorrow for sure.

M ☺

11

Under Pressure

SAM

THE MOVIE DATE didn't work out like I wanted. But when we're in school, Erica always has a smile on her face (although she laughs at too many of Foxxy's jokes) and she is really looking forward to NYC Nites.

Even with all that, I feel we're drifting apart, though. You don't have to be a rocket scientist to see things aren't going the way they should with Erica. If I could go back in time, I would not have suggested to Foxxy to join the art committee. But how was I to know Erica would start working with them, too?

Anyway, today I figure it's time to get Foxxy back with Holly Culver. After running into Holly, it's obvious she's not taking Foxxy back. She and Curt Goodwin are quite the couple these days.

So I'm desperate, just absolutely desperate, to get some advice and figure out a way to make things just a little bit smoother with Erica. But the only people I know who are in real relationships are Maureen and my parents.

I hate to do it, but I think I have little choice.

After school I spy on Maureen and Lutz. There's little to report:

Maureen: What do you want to watch?

Lutz: (grunts)

Maureen: Oh, this is supposed to be good.

Lutz: What is it?

Maureen: It's the movie with Emma Stone and Rachel McAdams and that guy who's in every movie. You know him.

Lutz: Robert Downey Jr.?

Maureen: No.

Lutz: Russell Crowe?

Maureen: No, the other guy. I'm sure you'll remember.

Lutz: Sean Penn?

Maureen: No, he's, like, in everything. I'm sure we'll see him soon.

(Silence)

Lutz: Are you hungry?

Maureen: No.

Lutz: I'm sort of hungry.

Maureen: We'll have dinner soon. And you know how my mom gets when she's cooking.

Lutz: (disappointed) I thought your dad was manning the grill tonight.

(At this point I have to do all I can not to yell at Lutz the Putz that he wasn't invited.)

Maureen: He has to work late.

Lutz: That's a bummer.

(Sharon enters, her face in a book)

Lutz: How's the English professor?

Sharon: I suppose you mean Duke.

Lutz: Yeah, Mr. Let-Me-Correct-Your-English.

Sharon: He's a lot like Mr. Darcy. Very complicated.

Maureen: Oh, here he is! What's his name?

Lutz: That's right. He is in everything. I forget his name. Isn't it, like, Henry Miller or something like that?

Me: (I've lost control) Bradley Cooper, you morons!

It was absolute torture watching and listening to those two. I don't know how Lutz does it. And what does Maureen see in him?

After dinner, a dinner in which Lutz had seconds and thirds and fourths until Dad said enough, I spied on my parents in the kitchen. My mother was on her computer and Dad was doing the dishes.

Mom: Did you pay the plumber?

Dad: Yeah.

Mom: Thanks.

Dad: (head in fridge) There's nothing to eat.

Mom: Have an apple.

Dad: I'm not in the mood for an apple. I want something sweet.

Mom: The apples are sweet.

Dad: I'm sort of in the mood for a pear.

Mom: I'll look for pears at the store.

(There's a long pause here. Then Dad grabs an apple and bites into it.)

Dad: Mmmmmm, this is sweet.

Mom: I told you.

(Another pause. I can't believe they're not talking about how much food Lutz ate.)

Dad: Will you get that bread I like when you go to the store? I think it's in a green bag.

Mom: Write it down on my list.

Dad writes SPECIAL BREAD on the shopping list and pats me on the head. How can he be in a good mood after Lutz has just eaten everything in the house? How can he be in a good mood with such a boring marriage?

Before I even have a chance to review and contemplate what this all means, Maureen's screams disrupt the peace of the house.

"I never want to see you again!"

Then the front door slams shut and we hear Maureen running up the steps.

Sharon enters the kitchen.

"What happened?" my mother asks.

"Maureen and Lutz had a fight," Sharon says.

Pass the popcorn. It's going to be fun watching Lutz try to get back in Maureen's good graces.

DUKE

Ralph Waldo looked different this morning.

"Good morning, Duke," he said. "Isn't it a lovely day?"

"I'm too busy to take note of such things," I replied, hoping he'd get the message I didn't have time to chat.

"Do you notice something different?" he asked.

"I have remarkable powers of deduction, Ralph. You should know that," I said, stalling for time, for though I knew something was different about him, I couldn't discern what it was.

Ralph did a little dance step and then it hit me. The cast on his leg was gone. His crutches were gone. Physically, he had been restored to his old self.

"Ta-da!" he said, pretending he was taking off a top hat. "And I'm happy to report I'll be ready to dance for the NYC Nights talent show!"

"That's very nice," I said. "Now if you'll excuse me, I'm very busy."

As I was walking away, he added, "Of course, now I only need a dance partner."

I ignored Ralph, though I was dying to turn back and glare at him, thinking perhaps even an obscene gesture would be apt, for I knew who that partner would be. No doubt he, the snake, had been planning to do something with Sharon for the talent stage. I'm man enough to admit that Ralph is an accomplished dancer. He can't sing, nor can he act, but he is a skilled dancer.

Thinking the answer to my Ralph Waldo dilemma could be found in the dusty pages of classic literature, I went immediately to the library. I didn't have to go past the letter A, and pulled from the shelf Jane Austen's *Pride and Prejudice*. It's been years since I've read it, but I recall it was a pretty good love story, and unlike most of the classics, the hero was not planted in a pine box at the end.

But then I spotted a copy of William Shakespeare's *Julius Caesar* (God forbid the librarians put the books in alphabetical order), which reminded me of the speech I would be giving during commencement. And knowing I'd be speaking to a packed house and everyone would be waiting on the edge of their seats made me even more anxious. But Duke Vanderbilt Samagura is not one to wilt under pressure. In fact, I thrive on it. And, full disclosure, I have been mentally preparing to give this address since the day I first graced the halls of Penn Valley.

I sat down to work in the library, but I hadn't gotten far when Sharon walked in.

Her eyes lit up as she approached me.

"Guess what?" she asked.

"I don't know," I said, smiling because Sharon's bright effervescence is so powerfully affecting.

"Ralph and I are going to do a tap-dance duet for the talent stage."

"Oh," I said.

Then I said, "Ah."

"Oh," I said once more.

I gathered my strength, for this information was quite a blow. A lesser man, I'm certain, would've been knocked off his feet.

"But what about us?" I asked. "I thought perhaps we could reprise our duet from the musical."

"Oh," she said. "We could still do something. Ralph is just a friend, Duke."

"That's wonderful," I lied. "Now if you'll excuse me, I have to get to work on my commencement speech."

"Of course," she said, adding, "I'd love to read it over and help if you'd like."

For some reason I bit my bottom lip, smiled (I probably looked as if I were in pain), and left Sharon with a "good day." I hurried away, knowing if I came across Ralph Waldo, he would surely end up using his crutches once again.

CHOLLIE

Billy's in love. She works at the pizzeria and her name is Angela.

"She's really an angel, Chollie. Wait till you get a load of her."

As Billy's talking about Angela, I'm thinking about my time with Miranda and it starts to make me really nervous. I realize that I've been losing that me-and-Miranda-dancing-in-the-moonlight feeling. Miranda is so busy planning all the end-of-the-year festivities, and baseball is really ramping up. So when we're in the library for lunch, even though it's just the two of us, we don't seem to talk much.

Like today we're in the library. I'm eating my lunch (roast beef with Swiss cheese, chips, a pickle, tomato soup, carrots, and a slice of chocolate cake) and Miranda is working on student council stuff.

"Do you have meat for lunch every day?" she asks.

"It depends," I say.

"What does it depend on?" she asks.

"I guess it depends on what's in the fridge. My mom makes my lunch. I don't ask for anything in particular; she just makes it."

"Interesting," she says.

But it's weird how she says it. I can't really explain except to say I think she was maybe making fun of me.

"And how're things with your little lady?" Billy says after he's done talking about Angela.

"Oh, it's all right," I say.

I think maybe it's true. Maybe it is all right. But then I think it's sort of like a math question, and it can go either way.

12
Freewriting

Sam Dolan

May 9th 2016

English 8A

Mr. Minkin

Suggested Writing Prompt: *What do you remember about your first day at Penn Valley Middle School? How did you feel at that time? How has your view of that first day changed? Explain.*

Hey Mr. Minkin,

It's crazy, really crazy, to think that was only two and a half years ago. The thing I remember most is how I thought Penn Valley was so big. I mean, I really didn't think I would ever find my way around even though my sister Maureen said it wouldn't be that hard at all. But coming from elementary school where everything is really small I guess it's just a natural reaction.

So there I was getting off the bus and now that makes me think how I was afraid of Ruben back then. Don't get me wrong, he still drives like a maniac but at least now when he says, "I gotta go!" I know what he's talking about.

I hate to admit it, but my sister Maureen helped me find my homeroom that first day. Mr. Howe was and still is my homeroom teacher and he was all business and told us the rules and gave us our locker numbers with the combinations which I was more excited about than anything else about going to middle school. Believe me, when you're coming from elementary school having a locker is a big deal. Then Mr. Howe gave us our schedules and I couldn't believe I had seven different classes with seven different teachers. I really thought that was pretty awesome.

Mr. Howe sent us off and I went to history class with Ms. Aguilar. I saw a lot of familiar faces as I walked to the back row and took a seat by the window. And then some dude comes along and takes the seat next to me and gives me a huge crazy smile. This dude just happened to be Jimmy Foxx, who quickly became my best buddy. Someone farted in class and Foxxy and I couldn't stop laughing. Ms. Aguilar had us step outside until we calmed down. And honestly I can remember that she wasn't really mad, she just wanted us to get a grip.

Foxxy and I formally introduced ourselves to each other while we were out there.

"Okay, ready to go back in?" Foxxy asked.

"Yeah," I said.

But before we had a chance to enter the classroom this big, hairy, ugly, smelly dude came up to us and started asking us all kinds of questions.

"What are you two doing out here?" he asks.

It's like the guy doesn't know we're in a school. He's totally shocked to see kids.

"My name is Lichtensteiner and I would suggest you two straighten up and fly right."

"Do we have a choice?" Foxxy asked.

"Let me tell you something. I got two sides. A bad side and a badder side."

Foxxy and I lost it all over again and just couldn't stop laughing.

Lichtensteiner didn't think it was funny at all.

He took us down to his office and gave us a long lecture and a bunch of detentions. Oh, and his office smelled like a tuna sandwich.

That's pretty much my first impression of Penn Valley. And let me tell you by the time I left Lichtensteiner's I felt like I'd been at Penn Valley forever.

Duke Vanderbilt Samagura

9 May 2016

English 8A

Mr. Minkin

Suggested Writing Prompt: *What do you remember about your first day at Penn Valley Middle School? How did you feel at that time? How has your view of that first day changed? Explain.*

Sir:

When I was at Myers Elementary the teachers talked about Penn Valley as if it were some mecca of higher learning. Within minutes, however, it was grossly apparent I was lied to.

I had my parents take me to school early since I did not want to rely on the shoddy school buses.

I arrived at Penn Valley before the doors were unlocked. Some school, right? Neal and Cassandra offered to wait with me but I shooed them away.

When the doors were finally opened I proceeded directly to the library, for I was in the midst of the final chapter of Oscar Wilde's <u>The</u>

<u>Picture of Dorian Gray</u>. (I'm sure you haven't heard of it, Mr. Minkin, but you might want to give it a try.) I was shocked to find the door to the library locked and lacking a sign indicating the library's hours. I turned and marched directly to the main office. I had a bone to pick.

The secretaries in the main office were shaking off the cobwebs from their undeserved summer slumber. A secretary greeted me.

"Good morning," she said.

"Oh, really?" I replied with great asperity. She didn't sense my outrage and anger and only seemed to be able to smile. Hopefully she could file papers as well or the taxpayers were getting ripped off.

"How can I help you?" she asked.

"You can help me by answering two questions. One, what time is the front door to the school unlocked in the morning? I had to wait at least fifteen minutes before I could enter the building. Two, why is the library not open prior to the start of classes? I should think many students would enjoy the peace and quiet of the library before they begin their toils at Penn Valley Middle School."

The secretary laughed and patted me on my head as if I were a mere child, as if I were cute instead of enraged.

"That was quite a list for the first day of school," she said.

"My dear lady," I replied. "I want answers."

That's when a man entered the reception area from his office. He raised his bushy eyebrows and approached me.

"What seems to be the matter, young man?"

"Aren't you curious whom you are addressing?" I asked him.

"Okay, what is your name and what is the matter?"

"My name is Duke Vanderbilt Samagura and according to your name tag, sir, you must be Mr. Lichtensteiner. I am here to get information and lodge two complaints. Firstly, what time can I enter the school? I am an early riser and have never slept past 7 A.M. in my life. And secondly, why is the library not open in the morning?"

Mr. Lichtensteiner, to his credit, took my concerns seriously. He stood tall and did not bend down to address me, which I greatly appreciated.

"The doors will generally be unlocked at 7:30. And the library is open before school but you must get a pass from Miss Rhoda, the librarian. We do this so that the library does not become a place for social gatherings."

I nodded slowly. I was beginning to like this Lichtensteiner but I didn't want to give away my hand.

"Now you'll have to excuse me. However, let me give you this pass. If there are any other concerns you can come to my office at 9:30. How does that sound?"

"Barely adequate," I answered. "Good day, sir," I added, turning on my heels to begin my career at Penn Valley Middle and my feeble attempt to make this school less of a laughingstock.

Miranda Mullaly

May 9, 2016

English 8A

Mr. Minkin

Suggested Writing Prompt: *What do you remember about your first day at Penn Valley Middle School? How did you feel at that time? How has your view of that first day changed? Explain.*

All we talked about in the fifth grade was how happy we'd be in middle school, with our own lockers and not being in the same building as kindergartners. But when I actually got here, I can remember being terribly nervous.

My father dropped me off at the front entrance next to the office. It seems weird now, but I think my initial thought was how big Penn Valley was. And it's funny because it seems so small to me now, almost cramped.

I remember being struck by the fact that I didn't know anyone. There must have been hundreds of students milling about and all of them looked like they knew where they were going, while I was wondering how I was going to find my way around the building.

There was a meeting for all the sixth graders in the auditorium. You could just feel the energy leaving the room. The principal (who I don't think I've seen since that day) spoke about how important the sixth grade was and she said it in this accusatory tone, almost as if we were all rotten to the core. So much for a friendly transition from elementary school to middle school.

After that we were sent to homeroom. My homeroom was with Mrs. Brown and even though I mapped it out the night before I just had no idea how I was going to find it. Should I make a left or right? Then I asked some boys walking by.

"Excuse me, could you please tell me where Mrs. Brown's room is?"

"There's no Mrs. Brown here," the boy said, laughing with his friends and not even stopping.

And his friend added, "You're in the wrong school."

And another said, "There's a Miss Scarlet and a Colonel Mustard and a Professor Plum, though."

Just thinking back on that makes me angry. I'm sure Charlie would never do something like that. He's such a gentleman. I wonder how he felt on his first day. I can't remember even seeing him in the sixth grade.

I finally found my homeroom and took a seat toward the back. I looked over at my classmates to see who I knew from elementary school and couldn't believe all the new faces. Then I looked at the girl next to me and smiled politely.

"Hi, I'm Miranda," I said.

"I'm Erica," she said.

"Nice to meet you," I said. "I had a hard time finding this room."

"Me too," Erica said. "And the kids weren't very friendly."

Erica and I had a laugh over that and have been good friends ever since.

Erica Dickerson

May 9, 2016

English 8A

Mr. Minkin

Suggested Writing Prompt: *What do you remember about your first day at Penn Valley Middle School? How did you feel at that time? How has your view of that first day changed? Explain.*

We had just moved to our new house, Mr. Minkin, in August and I didn't know a soul on my street. I missed my old friends from Harding Elementary, who were all going to Scott Middle School.

No surprise, I don't have rosy memories of my first day at Penn Valley. I can still remember how the school looked that day. The front lobby was very dark and it smelled like B.O. My older sisters, Rosie and Jane, were in the eighth grade then and they walked me to the auditorium. They didn't stay long because they were much more excited about going to a new school.

The auditorium seems pretty small now, but when you're a new student from a different town it's really scary. So many unfamiliar faces, and the worst part was that everyone, every single person in that auditorium, was having a conversation with someone else. I don't think I've ever felt more alone than at that moment.

But then things got a little better when I got to homeroom. That's where I met the coolest girl, Miranda, who would soon become my best friend.

We both were teased by some older kids about the teachers' names and the game Clue. Before we knew it we started making our own little game of Clue with the map of the school and teachers' names and classroom supplies. The homeroom meeting was kind of long and by the time we were done we actually had a game put together. And although not everyone would admit it, I know it helped us remember all the teachers' names and where the classrooms were.

I don't know if it was the angle of the sun or if the lights weren't working in the morning, but when I met Rosie and Jane after school in the lobby, it wasn't nearly as dark as it was when I arrived that morning.

Chollie Muller

May 9, 2016

English 8A

Mr. Minkin

Suggested Writing Prompt: *What do you remember about your first day at Penn Valley Middle School? How did you feel at that time? How has your view of that first day changed? Explain.*

Dear Mr. Minkin,

My first day at Penn Valley was very inauspicious. (Did I use that word right? Miranda has been helping me with my vocab.)

The reason it was inauspicious is because I lost track of time. When I got to school everyone was hanging out by the field next to the gym. And everyone told me that we didn't have to report to class until the first bell rang. I knew right then and there I was going to love Penn Valley Middle School.

Within no time we got a football game going, nothing very serious, just a game of touch with an emphasis on passing the ball. The game was so good we really didn't notice when the bells rang.

The best part was that there were some eighth graders playing and Bobby Kelly, who's in high school now and playing on the varsity team, was covering me. After I beat him for a touchdown (it was a diving catch) he held out his hand and helped me up.

He said, nice catch, kid, and I said, thanks.

Then Coach (I didn't know who he was then) came outside and called everybody in. That's when I found out everyone I was playing with had gym first period and I was supposed to be in the sixth grade meeting in the auditorium but I was late.

When I got into the school the hallways were completely empty. It was kind of creepy and would have been a great setup for a scary movie.

I had to pass by the office to get to the auditorium, and that's when I was stopped by Mr. Lichtensteiner.

"What happened to you?" he said.

I looked down at my shirt and pants. The

shirt was ripped and pretty dirty and I was sweating through it. My pants had so many grass stains they looked green.

"I was playing outside," I said.

"You know what you are?" he asked.

I shook my head.

"You're late," he said. "And that'll cost you two detentions. Do you know who I am?"

I shook my head.

"I'm Mr. Lichtensteiner, and I run this school. I suggest you stay on my good side."

I took Mr. Lichtensteiner's advice and went right into the auditorium.

Anyway, that was my first day, Mr. Minkin. And even though it was an inauspicious beginning (love that word) I served my two detentions and I haven't been in trouble since.

13

The Final Stretch

DUKE

Perhaps the only good thing about having two parents who are college professors is that the house is filled with books. And it's even better having parents who are sociology professors, for that means the books have not been read and are in pristine condition.

William Safire's[24] *Lend Me Your Ears* has been my constant companion (sorry, Jane Austen, but *Pride and Prejudice* is up next). *Lend Me Your Ears*, if you haven't read it, is a compilation of many of the world's great speeches. If you

....

24. Renowned *New York Times* columnist who wrote the influential column On Language.

happen to be called upon to give a speech, a dedication, or even a eulogy, don't hesitate to peruse this volume. It has been invaluable to me through the years.

Needless to say, thanks to this incomparable tome, I was full of confidence before auditioning for the commencement speech. As Dizzy Dean[25] said, it ain't bragging if you can do it, and I was prepared to do it.

As I began the final stretch of the eighth grade, my grades were superb, I felt assured I could put the finishing touches on NYC Nights, and Sharon and I would soon begin practicing our routine for NYC Nights in earnest. All was well.

The auditions were held after school in Mr. Porter's room. I arrived promptly and took a seat near the back, flanked by Knuckles and Moose, just in case there was trouble. While I reviewed my notes and patiently waited, the door opened and Mr. Lichtensteiner entered. He smiled upon us as if we were his subjects. Knuckles and Moose fidgeted nervously. Poor fellows, I know they've been terribly bored.

"Good afternoon, everyone," Mr. Lichtensteiner began. "I am here with some very good news. Because there

---

25. One of the greatest baseball pitchers, who was later well-known for his homespun adages as a baseball announcer.

has been some controversy over the years regarding commencement speakers, we've decided to pick the name out of a hat this year. That seems fairest, doesn't it?"

I shot up to my feet faster than an attorney making an objection.

"What is fair about that?" I asked.

"Good question, young man. And your name?"

Why does this man keep forgetting my name? I've been practically running the school for three years.

"My name, sir, is Duke Vanderbilt Samagura. I am the student council president."

"Pleasure to meet you, Mr. Duke," he said. "So, let's begin."

"You didn't answer my question," I said. "How is it fair to pick out of a hat rather than have a competition and have the best man or woman win?"

"If there's a competition, then it is not fair to those who are not chosen, don't you agree?" he asked.

"No, I don't. And anyway, if that's the case, why don't we let the student council president give the speech?"

"Again, that would be unfair as well. Parents would complain that their son or daughter didn't get to speak at the commencement because their son or daughter was not the student council president. My phone literally rings off the hook this time of year."

"Mine too," Mr. Porter unwisely interjected.

"So it's quite obvious that in the spirit of fairness for all involved, we shall pick the name out of the hat."

"The enormity[26] of this decision proves the gross incompetence of you and your ilk!" I said.

"Yes, it was a very large, very big decision,"[27] Lichtensteiner replied.

I didn't know what to say after that. I was speechless (pun intended!), and here just minutes before I had been prepared to give an unforgettable address that people would be talking about for years to come.

Believe it or not, and probably simply due to the mind-numbing experience of attending this poor excuse of a school, I actually gave up for a moment and thought that my odds, at 10 percent, weren't that bad.

We wrote our names on index cards, folded them twice, and dropped them into the hat which Lichtensteiner held in his hand. Then he picked out a card, smiled, and said, "Congratulations, Ralph Waldo."

26. A monstrous offense or evil; an outrage. I have even heard President Obama incorrectly use this word, a mark against his alma mater, Columbia University.

27. Please do not miss footnote 26. For future generations, please learn this word.

Everyone looked, but Ralph Waldo was not in the room. I jumped up from my seat.

"I move we pick another name from the hat," I said, then added so that Lichteinsteiner, the numskull, could comprehend my request, "since he isn't here. After all, it wouldn't be fair to us all who are here."

"It's okay," Mr. Porter, the overly officious jerk, unwisely responded. "I promised Ralph I'd enter his name. He's practicing for his NYC Nights routine. I'll tell him the good news."

"Excellent," Mr. Lichtensteiner said, smiling like he'd actually done some work. "Thank you, everyone, for giving it your best."

Then he turned to leave the room. I stood up again.

"Um, just a moment, sir," I said.

Lichtensteiner paused at the door, giving Knuckles and Moose the extra seconds needed to thrash him.

I left the room, quite discouraged, only stopping to tell Knuckles and Moose not to forget about Mr. Porter.

To say I left the room angry would be an understatement. I was livid. I was enraged.

If I was my old self, I would have left the school, gone home to my room, and contemplated the whole monstrous affair. Instead, I entered the auditorium to check on the progress for NYC Nights. As you can see, I have evolved and matured as a person.

Outside the auditorium I caught the melody to Joplin's "The Entertainer," and I think I can state here that for a moment, just one moment, my spirits were lifted. After all, I thought, how can I let the administration's malfeasance get me down? Why should I expect anything more? I didn't exactly chuckle, but a smile did cross my face. I was the student council president. I was respected. And we were about to pull off a wonderful event despite the idiocy which surrounded us.

When I entered the auditorium, however, all hope was gone.

I stopped and looked at the stage. Sharon was in the arms of Ralph Waldo. He was teaching her to tap-dance.

And there to the right of the stage was a large poster, the wet paint still drying.

PENN VALLEY CELEBRATES NYC NITES!

It was seeing "NITES" that did it, I think. It was that misspelling that drove me to the edge.

"No! No! No! No!" I screamed.

As I walked down the aisle with purpose in my stride and fire in my eyes, everyone stopped. Ralph, the chump, actually ran from the stage. Sharon stood alone on the stage (I should've been at her side) and watched me with, I'm sorry to report, horror.

I ripped the drying poster from the wall. I tore it and shredded it into a thousand pieces, screaming again and again, "That's not how you spell 'NIGHTS'! That's not how you spell 'NIGHTS'! That's not how you spell 'NIGHTS'!"

After I finished, my hands stinging with fresh paper cuts, I stopped. The auditorium was silent. My peers were, no doubt, embarrassed for me. Even Knuckles and Moose, fresh from thrashing Mr. Porter, averted their eyes from me.

"That's not how you spell 'nights,'" I said after a pause, my voice now a whisper.

I kicked the shredded papers and left the auditorium as some joker, probably Sam Dolan, asked, "How do you spell 'nights'?"

CHOLLIE

Coach calls me and the guys into his office first thing this morning.

"Listen, fellows, we've been too uptight. We're going

to take the day off, get our heads ready for the Cedarbrook game."

Everyone looks very confused, and then they stare at me. I know what they're wondering. I raise my hand.

"Coach, what are you saying?"

"We need a day off to clear our heads. No practice this afternoon. Don't think about the Cedarbrook game, not until tomorrow at least."

Since I'm the captain, I don't cheer and show excitement like the other guys, but this is really perfect. This will give me a chance to go to the student council meeting and see how things are shaping up for NYC Nites. And I'll get to finally spend some time with Miranda. We've both been so incredibly busy it's hard to believe. But pretty soon we'll be finished and we'll have the NYC Nites celebration with the talent show and the art exhibit and the food and all that. It's the perfect end to the year.

I also really need the break because Billy and my mom are going at it. You see, Billy has a new girlfriend, Angela, and he's been spending so much time with her that he quit the job at the pizza shop. Billy says he quit, but Mom says he got fired, and it sounds like a little bit of both. It doesn't really matter what happened, though, because Mom has a policy that Billy can't stay at the house if he doesn't have a job. So, obviously, I have a lot on my mind.

At lunch Miranda is so busy we don't get a chance to talk about anything except for the big night. And she has really taken over a lot of responsibilities.

"Did you hear about Duke?" she asks.

"No, did he break his leg in a skiing accident?" I ask.

Miranda laughs. "No," she says. "He flipped out yesterday and started ripping up the signs for NYC Nites. I think the pressure finally got to him."

"Wow," I say. I miss a lot when we're in the middle of baseball. Now I'm really glad I have the afternoon off.

"It was pretty crazy. So I promised Mr. Porter I'd take on some extra responsibility. In fact, I promised I'd stop by his room to go over some things. Sorry I can't have lunch with you."

"That's okay because we don't have practice today. So I'll see you at the student council meeting."

"Perfect," she says. "I'll see you then."

I have to say Coach really knows what he's doing because when I get to the auditorium after school, I feel super relaxed. And I just have this great feeling come over me, not only because I'll see Miranda but also because I know I'm going to rip the cover off the ball when we play Cedarbrook.

Miranda gets right down to business the moment everyone is in the auditorium.

"Okay, let's get started. We have two weeks until NYC Nites. So we're going to hear some updates from the committees and then we'll get right back to work. Let's hear how the entertainment committee is coming along. Sam?"

Sam Dolan says, "Yeah."

"What do we have booked for the entertainment?" Miranda asks.

Sam says "um" about fifty times.

"Okay, we'll come back to entertainment. How're things coming along with the spirit committee?"

Everyone looks around, but there doesn't seem to be a spirit committee.

"What happened to the spirit committee?" Miranda asks, and I can tell from her voice she's starting to get upset.

Jimmy Foxx finally stands up. "I think the spirit committee is all spirited out after what happened yesterday. Sharon has to redo all the posters."

This gets some of the people laughing, but Miranda only becomes more upset. She takes a deep breath and looks over at Mr. Porter. He's asleep.

"How is the art exhibit coming along?"

Jimmy Foxx holds up a painting.

"That is disturbing," Miranda says. And that's really the only way to describe it. It's dark, just a lot of black paint with some red paint that looks like dripping blood.

"Good," Jimmy Foxx says. "It's supposed to be. It matches my heart."

Miranda moves along after checking her clipboard.

"How're things coming along with the food committee?" She asks this very slowly, sort of like she knows what the answer is but doesn't want to hear it.

Stephen Jones stands up.

"How are the donations from the restaurants coming along?" she asks.

"They all said no."

"When?"

"I guess about four weeks ago," he says.

"Charlie," she says. "What about the pizzas?"

This is kind of like the lawyer show Billy likes to watch, when the lawyer is asking whoever is on the stand a question and they know the answer is going to save the day. But this time my answer is not going to save the day.

"Um, about the pizzas. You see, my brother isn't really working there anymore," I say.

That's all Miranda can take.

"I don't get it! What's wrong with you people? You all

chose NYC Nites over putting on a dance. We made a commitment to this entire school, to this community, to the Penn Valley Vegetarian Society, to ourselves! We made a promise that we would have this special night. And now no one is willing to do any of the work. How can you all be content letting this happen?"

By this point Miranda looks more disappointed than mad. She lets out a gasp and starts to tear up. She takes her clipboard and throws it across the auditorium. And then she storms out, not even bothering to look at me.

I feel really terrible. So much for a stress-free afternoon.

Billy makes me feel even worse when I give him the update. He's packing up his clothes because he's going to stay with his friends back at college. I always get a little sad when he leaves, even though I'm sure he'll be back in a month.

"What's up, big guy?" he asks.

I tell him about the whole thing, every single thing I can think of. Billy takes it all in and rubs his chin. He's quiet for about one whole minute, which for Billy is a seriously long time. He's been known to talk at funerals.

"Okay, here's what I think, and I don't want you to get mad when I tell you, got it?"

"Sure, Billy," I say. "I think I really need your advice on this one."

"It's over," he says.

"What's over?" I ask. "You and Angela?"

"No, you and Miranda."

I don't know what to say to this. Is he serious?

"Are you serious?"

"Absolutely." He leans forward, the way Coach does when he's drawing up a play. "You had a good run, right? But the school year is almost over. You don't even have a dance to worry about anymore. And you're going to want to be a free agent going into the summer and starting high school."

I begin to feel a little bit sick to my stomach. I wasn't expecting this. And I'm pretty sure I'd rather be with Miranda than be a free agent.

I stand, sort of in a daze. As I'm leaving his room, Billy calls out.

"One more thing," he says. "You'll probably want to end it before she does so you don't look like the loser. My advice is to do it fast, like ripping off a Band-Aid."

As I'm lying in bed, thinking about this whole big mess with Miranda, I also remember the championship game.

How am I going to hit a baseball and field my position with all this craziness on my mind?

SAM

There's been an outbreak of some kind at Penn Valley. I'm no doctor, but you don't have to study medicine to see something's wrong. After yesterday's insanity with Duke attacking poster boards, I didn't think things could get any weirder. But then today Miranda Mullaly shows the world how much she hates clipboards and embarrasses herself by crying in front of the whole student council. This is a crazy place, Penn Valley Middle School.

At first I thought it was all pretty funny, but it seems like everyone is trying to make an effort now. Erica chases after Miranda when she (Miranda, not Erica) has a meltdown. Foxxy goes off with all his new artsy friends, like Terri and Jenny, and they start painting like crazy, trying to fill the art exhibit. And Ralph Waldo and Sharon show up and start redoing posters. I figure I should get to work on something for the talent show and start thinking of who else I can ask to perform besides Ralph and Sharon. Otherwise, this show's going to be a dud.

When Erica comes back, she's mad at me.

"What did you do that for?" she asks.

"I did nothing," I say.

"Exactly. You did nothing. Did you even try to get entertainment? What have you been doing this whole time I've been helping Foxxy?"

First of all, what did people think the entertainment committee was going to do? Did they really think we were going to book Adele or Kanye West to come and perform at Penn Valley? I mean, come on, people. I don't say any of this, of course.

Instead I say, "I thought we could do a little entertaining."

She laughs, then points at Ralph and Sharon. "They better be prepared to dance for about three hours because *we got nothing!*"

Erica leaves, but she doesn't destroy anything or cry, so I guess she doesn't have whatever disease Duke and Miranda are suffering from. But still.

Now that I think about it, I'm not mad at Erica but at her buddy Miranda. I really don't need her berating me. Who does she think she is, Duke?

Oh, and thanks a whole lot, Miranda, because of your temper tantrum, Erica is mad at me. Come to think of it, I'm mad about this whole NYC Nites thing. What were we thinking? What is NYC Nites anyway? We could've just had a dance instead. And I missed out on playing baseball because of all this. If I had a time machine, I'd go back and fight for the dance. NYC Nites is a stupid idea.

I'm so mad that if I had anything written down for NYC Nites, I'd probably tear it all up.

14

Surprise!

DUKE

I've been under the radar since my little outburst in the auditorium. It's been quite nice, in a way. I've been able to study for my exams, and for the first time in years, I've gone home directly after the end of the school day. One cannot burn the candle at both ends for too long, and I'm man enough to admit I needed rest.

But after two days, I was ready to face the music, if you will, and make the final push for the end of the school year.

I also now find myself in a very difficult position. In a pickle, as Cassandra is wont to say.[28] In recent weeks, Sharon and I have drifted apart. It's not hard to see why.

---

28. I doubt she knows this particular colloquialism comes from Shakespeare's *The Tempest* (act 5, scene 1). And I simply don't have the time to educate her.

I'm older and more mature and have responsibilities most could barely dream of.

It has also become clear that Sharon is not the great intellect I thought she was. For example, once I mentioned the presidential election in November and expressed my opinion that the voting age should be lowered to fourteen (if one could, of course, pass a rigorous test), and Sharon looked at me in astonishment.

"Who cares?"

"I beg your pardon?" I could hardly believe my ears. Nor, for that matter, could I believe my eyes. For the first time I could actually see that Sharon and Sam are related. Their eyes (blue) and hair (sandy brown) are both the same color.

"The idea of having a fourteen-year-old vote is absurd and you know it."

"I don't think it's absurd to participate in the American republic," I said defensively.

"No, you don't really think that," she said.

"Is that so?" I asked. "And, pray tell, how would you know if I felt that way or not?"

"Because just last week you said the opposite. When you were complaining about the delays in building the new wing of the high school, you said the problem was that too many numskulls had too much to say. You said voting should be limited to those over the age of forty and only to those who could prove they had paid taxes for ten years."

I was nonplussed.[29] Did I really say that? And did Sharon really remember word for word what I said? It did sound vaguely familiar.

I struggled for something to say but drew a blank.

I stood up.

"Where are you going?" she asked.

"I suddenly don't feel well," I told her.

You see, it's clear that our relationship had run its course. When I left her and the library, I knew it was over. Now I had to find a way to let her down easily.

After dinner I sat at my computer, trying to write a few scenarios illustrating how the breakup would carry itself out. But, for the first time in my life, I couldn't write.

I went for a contemplative constitutional, but upon my return, once again, I drew a blank.

Finally I lay in bed, eyes on the ceiling until my heavy eyelids closed.

When I arrived at school this morning, I felt a little bit better. Maybe we just needed some space.

....

29. Put at a loss as to what to think, say, or do; bewildered; speechless.

I found her in the library before classes started.

"Oh, hi, Duke," Sharon said, smiling as if our troubles were in the past.

"Good morning, Sharon." I took a seat across from her.

"I'm glad you're here," she said. "I've been wanting to talk to you, but I didn't want to say what I have to say over the phone."

"Okay," I said. "What is it?"

"First, I want to tell you how much fun the last two months have been," she said.

"I'm certainly glad you have enjoyed them."

"And I want you to know that I think you're a really great guy," she continued.

"And I think you're a fine young woman," I said.

"Please, let me finish. This is not easy for me."

Sharon stopped there and I was getting the feeling she was going to break up with me. I waited.

"I don't think we should see each other anymore. I just don't think it's working out. I feel as if we're drifting apart."

She paused. No, I quickly realized, she had stopped. It was my turn to talk. My turn to beg. My turn to plead. My turn to cry for her to come back. I would, of course, do no such thing. Duke Vanderbilt Samagura is made of sterner stuff.

"But we can still be friends," she added hastily, as if it had just come into her mind.

Suddenly I envisioned myself dateless at the NYC Nights celebration, standing alone on the stage. Music playing and me standing there, lost without Sharon in my arms, like some nerd dancing in front of the mirror in his room. It was an out-of-body experience and I had to shake my head in order to focus on Sharon. I wished for the nightmare to end.

Then I begged. "Oh, no, please, give me another chance. I can change. Please, just tell me what I did wrong."

Then I bargained. "Let's just give it a day or two, shall we? I don't think we should make final decisions so early in the morning."

Then came the tears.

SAM

Nothing surprises me anymore.

Lutz and Maureen got back together. Just like they do every time they break up.

What else? Oh yeah, Erica dumped me. But again, not surprising. I mean, I always thought she was going to be my future ex-girlfriend.

In case you can't tell, that's sarcasm. The reality is I

feel worse than I have ever felt in the history of my life.

Worse than the time I nailed Mr. Mullaly in the face with a snowball.

Worse than when Foxxy and I messed up our trip to the museum and we accidentally set off those alarms.

It all happens in the auditorium, which is fitting, because it's really where our relationship began, when we were in the musical together.

Erica and I are alone and I'm trying out my jokes and she's watching. Sort of like what we've been doing for quite a bit.

"Sam," she says, "I think we should talk."

Now, no one has ever said "I think we should talk" to me before. But I turn instantly cold, kind of like there's a ghost in the auditorium. I mean, it's freezing cold. And I'm on the stage and Erica is sitting in the first row, so I have to walk down the steps to be next to her. I practically limp going down the stairs, as if my legs are brittle. I'll bet this is the way people feel when they climb Mount Everest.

"I've been wanting to talk to you, Sam," she says when I plop down next to her.

"Me too," I laugh. "I've really been focusing on the talent stage, honest. I have at least three people signed up and I was thinking I could emcee and—"

"I don't think we should go out anymore," she says.

That's one thing about Erica Dickerson: she certainly doesn't beat around the bush.

I'm sort of panicking in a way. I worry I'm going to forget to breathe. Isn't that weird? I mean, the last thing I want to do is faint.

"I realize now that when I thought I was in love with you," Erica says, "I was actually in like with you."

"*In like* with me?"

"Yeah. I *like* you a lot, Sam. You're funny and you always make me smile. I hope we can be friends forever."

"*In like* with me," I say again. "What does that even mean? Are there any *like* songs? Is there such a thing as a *like* story?"

Erica holds my hand. But it's not in a nice way. It's sort of the way my parents used to hold my hand when we were crossing the street. Not romantic at all.

"You know, Sam, I think you like me too."

"This is all pretty confusing," I say. Then there's a long pause and we stare at each other. I bet if someone saw us, they would say we were *in love* and not *in like*. "So I guess you're not my girlfriend anymore?"

"I don't think so."

And just like that, I became the big loser Lutz predicted I'd be. How the heck does he still have a girlfriend and I don't?

"What about the NYC Nites?" I ask.

"I still think we can pull it off. Everyone is working really hard now. And we can definitely still hang out!"

"What about the talent stage? Do you still want to do a skit together?"

"I'd love to."

I have to think about this.

"But not as boyfriend and girlfriend."

"Nope. Something better. We'll be two friends onstage. We've always been friends, really, all this time."

CHOLLIE

I sure wish Billy wouldn't have said anything about breaking up with Miranda. I'm definitely not going to break up with her, but when Billy makes the suggestion, it plants a seed in my brain that Miranda is going to break up with me.

I just can't get it out of my head now. I even start thinking that we're not a good match. She's always doing work for NYC Nites and getting good grades and making the world a better place by being a vegetarian. And here I am, playing baseball and floating by with my classwork and eating meat. So if she starts thinking this way, I'm doomed. But I don't want it to end. Even if we don't have much in common, I just really like being with her.

When I get to school this morning, I'm super tired and nervous about Miranda and I'm going crazy thinking about the game.

Somehow I get through the day. I hardly see Miranda. And for lunch I tell Miranda I have to go to Coach's office, but instead I sneak down to the locker room and eat my lunch alone in a smelly corner.

Finally the day ends and I get to hit the field. For once, even though there's tons of pressure with the game and Coach is a nut, I actually feel relaxed. It's almost like I can catch my breath, if that makes sense.

It's really a great game, too. And there's a great crowd. Almost the whole school, it seems. I don't see Miranda, but Mr. Mullaly is there.

We go back and forth, trading leads, and both teams are playing their best. There isn't an error committed by either side and we even turn a double play, which isn't easy to do.

At the top of the seventh, we have the lead, seven to six. And when we take the field, we all know we just need three outs to win the game. We get two players out, but they still have guys on second and third. So this is it. If we can get the final out, we win!

I have every scenario going through my head. Any ball

hit to me and I have to go to first base for the final out and we win. If they get a hit, our outfielder has to go home with it to try to get the go-ahead run out at home plate.

And that's exactly what happens. A line drive is hit, and I dive for it but can't reach it. It's hard enough for Jason Lewis to get the second guy out at home, so we're tied once again.

We go back to the dugout pretty excited about the throw at home. And we know we just need one run to win the game. Eddie Naves is up first and I'm second. I can't help it, but I just get it into my mind that I'm going to hit a home run. I've stayed awake at night dreaming about this situation and now I have the chance.

As I'm taking some warm-up swings, Eddie jumps on the first pitch and hits a double down the line. Crazy as this might sound because of my past troubles in pressure situations, I actually feel confident going up to the plate. This is what I've been dreaming of, and here it is. I just know I'm going to win the game.

I dig in at the plate and feel pretty loose, I really do.

The pitcher looks in for his sign, then looks at Eddie on second.

"Time!" the umpire yells.

I step out of the batter's box and I see that it's Coach

who has called time-out. I run up the third-base line to talk strategy.

"I think you need to lay down a bunt," he whispers.

"A bunt?"

"Yeah. There's no outs. Let's try to get Eddie to third."

"But I can hit this guy," I say.

"Trust me, get the bunt down and get Eddie to third."

It's true Eddie isn't the fastest guy in the world, but if I hit a home run, it doesn't matter.

But Coach is right. I get the bunt down, and almost beat out the throw. As I'm walking back to the dugout, everyone's politely clapping but not cheering. And again I look for Miranda but I can't find her.

I get high fives in the dugout, and a second later Ernie Williams hits a single and Eddie Naves comes home with the winning run. It's pretty awesome, finally celebrating a big win. We put Coach on our shoulders and carry him off the field.

When we run off the field, I wave to my parents and Mr. Mullaly, but I don't see Miranda. I just can't explain how I feel. Even though we finally won, for some reason I feel like I lost.

15

A State of Confusion

DUKE

I, Duke Vanderbilt Samagura, have not been myself of late. I think the stress has finally caught up to me. I need a break. I'm certain my doctor would prescribe a week on a pond with a fishing pole.

Sharon put the dagger in my heart on Friday. This week I've avoided her and the rest of my classmates, even to the point of shirking my responsibilities and leaving school after classes were over. I honestly couldn't go on and needed to regroup.

Unfortunately, I do not live a life conducive to relaxation. I am a man constantly on the move. And so this morning, when Neal and Cassandra suggested we go to the

Penn Valley Mall, I quickly agreed. I needed to get out and away from my thoughts of Sharon.

Neal and Cassandra, who have practically ignored me my entire life, have been suddenly struck by this incurable desire to spend time with me, to know about me, to, in short, make up for years of bad parenting.

"You're growing so big and strong I don't think any of your dress shirts fit you any longer," Cassandra said when we entered the mall.

I wanted to be alone. I wanted to be ignored. I had to ditch them somehow.

Neal added, with an insufferable smile, "And you'll want to look your best for the NYC Nights celebration."

Of course, I hadn't told Neal and Cassandra about my breakup with Sharon. The last thing I needed was for them to find out what happened. I didn't want sympathy or empathy or even someone to talk to. I could not handle Neal, who has learned everything about parenthood from what he has seen on television, calling me "pal" or "kiddo" or "slugger."

I looked at my surroundings. The mall is an emporium of junk food, a castle of the mundane and banal, a fortress of the very worst of America. Its only saving grace, however, is MacFadden's Boutique, a fine shop which not only carries the best bow ties, but an array of ascots, cuff links, and Jeff caps, along with suspenders galore.

At MacFadden's I felt different. Whenever I'm in this spectacular shop, I am like the proverbial kid in the candy store. It's as if I've traveled in a time machine to better days, days when men took pride in what they wore, days when men used a walking cane (I'd love to use one of those to straighten out Ralph Waldo), days when teachers dressed better than in running sneakers and blue jeans. Days, in short, when people cared.

I took my time admiring the bow ties, though I knew in my mind what I wanted to wear. As student council president, of course, I should wear Penn Valley's colors, and my eyes instantly fell upon a gorgeous blue-and-gold bow tie. It was perfect for NYC Nites.[30]

After we paid for the bow tie and had it wrapped, I told my parents I'd like to stroll around the bookstore. They were more than eager to abandon me to shop. They actually like the mall.

"We'll meet you at the bookstore, say, in an hour," Cassandra said.

They were off, holding hands like high-school sweethearts. Pathetic!

On my way to the bookstore, I heard voices and

....
30. I have given up my battle to spell words correctly.

laughter to my left. I stopped and saw Sam Dolan and Erica Dickerson across the arcade. I watched them from afar, even hiding behind an advertisement[31] so they wouldn't see me.

They were having so much fun it was infectious, and they made all the people around them smile. Chollie Muller and Miranda Mullaly were not far behind, in a similar state of glee.

Was the world going mad?

I'd never experienced an emotional roller coaster quite like this. Part of me wanted to have Knuckles and Moose break up their fun. Another part of me wanted to tell the security guard to escort them off the premises for disturbing the peace with their incessant laughter. And still another part of me knew it was pure envy. I knew deep down in my heart my feelings were childish.

I walked to the bookstore, rather quickly lest my classmates see me. I felt relieved to be among the stacks, and it was almost refreshing to be alone.

I don't know what it was that attracted me to the children's section of the bookstore. I hadn't been there

---

31. To add to my disgrace, the advertisement was for *La Saison des Jonquilles*. Believe it or not, it's still playing. Perhaps I'll watch it alone.

since, well, I suppose since I was a child. When you're reading Dickens at the age of nine, there isn't much in the YA, middle grade, or picture book section that appeals.

But there I was, surrounded by thousands of titles many of my classmates couldn't put down. I decided, what the heck, maybe I'll grab a couple to just see what all the fuss is about.

On my way to the checkout counter, I bumped into, of all people, Sharon Dolan.

At first I tried to escape behind a bookshelf, but Sharon greeted me.

"Hi, Duke," she said.

"Good day, Sharon," I said. "What do you have there?"

She held up a copy of *Sense and Sensibility*.

"Is that for you?"

"My old copy has actually fallen apart," she said.

"I didn't know you were a fan of Austen," I said.

"Duke, I read for pleasure, not to tell people what I have read."

What a profound statement.

"What do *you* have there?" she asked.

"Oh, nothing," I said, putting the book under my arm.

"Duke, let me see," she said.

I was silent as she took the book from me.

She looked at me with curiosity, as if I'd just said something she didn't comprehend. I think at that moment she knew me, Duke Vanderbilt Samagura, better than I knew myself.

"*The Giver*," she said. She held the book in her delicate hands and looked up at me. She looked directly into my eyes. And her eyes sparkled. Slowly a knowing smile came across her face.

"Oh, Duke," she said. "Poor Duke."

I stood there, unable to move, alone, more alone than I had ever felt in my life. Even with Sharon in front of me, smiling and holding the book, nodding as if a mystery had been solved. She wasn't angry, thankfully, just a bit curious.

I was so filled with emotion I wasn't sure if I was going to laugh or cry.

Finally I made a noise. Laughter?

"What's so funny?" Sharon asked.

"I am," I answered. "But you already know that."

SAM

I'm confused. I mean, I am seriously confused.

Erica doesn't say anything to anyone at school about breaking up with me. I know this because Foxxy would be talking about it. And you sure can bet Lichtensteiner would say something about it.

So it has been a really strange and quiet week. I feel like an invisible man and no one even asks me where I've been when I don't show up for NYC Nites planning meetings.

And then on Friday night I get a phone call. I'm in my room when my mom tells me the phone is for me.

"Hello?" I say.

"Hi, Sam. It's Erica."

"Oh, hi, Erica," I say. My heart starts racing. Is she calling to tell me she has reconsidered dumping me?

"What are you doing tomorrow?" she asks.

"Saturday?"

"Yes," she laughs. "What are you doing tomorrow, Saturday?"

"Nothing . . ."

"Want to go to the mall with me? I have an idea for NYC Nites."

"I guess," I say. It's all happening so fast I don't know what to think.

"Great. I'll meet you there tomorrow at noon. At the food court, okay?"

"Is Foxxy going to be there?"

"Not unless you invite him," she says.

"Perfect. I'll see you there."

So we meet in the food court. I'm a little surprised to see Chollie and Miranda there with Erica. We all say hi and all that, then Chollie and I get slices of pizza while Erica and Miranda slurp down these huge coffee drinks that look like they're almost all whipped cream. Then Erica tells us about her idea.

"What we're going to do today is get some material for the talent show. We're going to ask some random people if they have any special talents. And we'll videotape them and play it at NYC Nites, just in case we have some extra time."

"I still don't get it," I say.

"Let's take you as an example, okay?"

She pulls out her smartphone and hands it to Miranda. Miranda starts videoing Erica as she speaks into the camera.

"We're here at the Penn Valley Mall in search of special talents that Penn Valley residents are hiding from us. Here we have a young man who appears to be especially talented at devouring pizza."

The camera is on me, and my mouth is full of pizza.

"Excuse me, sir. But we have been watching you eat this pizza and we are amazed. How did you learn to eat pizza like this?"

I'm going to lose it. I start laughing and just can't help

it. I put my hand out to cover the camera because I am seconds away from spitting out all the half-chewed pizza in my mouth. Finally I get the pizza down and drink some soda and catch my breath.

"We thought we were going to lose you there," Miranda says.

I laugh again. I can't even talk, I'm laughing so hard.

"Are we ready to get some material?" Erica asks.

This is a great idea. Isn't Erica hilarious?

She takes the lead and I'm amazed at how many people stop and chat with her. Erica just has a special way about her. We meet a guy who can stop a fan with his tongue (gross but funny) and a lady who can play a song by Bach with her toes on the mall piano. After a couple of hours, we have tons of material and I don't know if I've honestly ever had more fun.

I'm still bummed that Erica isn't my girlfriend, but I'm certainly glad she's my friend.

CHOLLIE

Miranda asks me if I want to go to the mall with her on Saturday so she can get some things for NYC Nites. I'm not sure what this means, and I don't say anything to Billy. But it doesn't seem like Miranda would ask me to go to the mall with her just so she could dump me, does it?

I meet up with Miranda and Erica and Sam in the food court, and Erica tells us her idea of filming funny interviews for the talent stage. We go along with Sam and Erica and have fun, but then Miranda and I head to all the stores to try to get gift certificates and things like that, as prizes for the show.

Asking for free stuff is hard, but Miranda is incredibly persistent.

After hitting just about every store, Miranda and I plop down on a bench to rest.

"Thanks, Charlie," she says.

"For what?" I ask.

"For being here. I really needed this."

"Sure," I say.

"My father told me what you did at the baseball game."

I think about the game. This might sound crazy, but I feel better about it now than when it happened. I really wanted to hit a home run, but winning as a team was just as important. And it's so much better thinking about the game and knowing Miranda is interested.

"Didn't you want to knock him in?" she asks.

"Of course," I say. "But we just needed that one run

and Coach wanted me to do that, so that's what you do, for the team."

"I'm sorry I wasn't there," she says. "I was just so embarrassed about what happened in the auditorium."

Miranda has tears in her eyes when she says this.

"It's okay, really, it's all right."

She nods and puts her head on my shoulder.

"I have to admit, though, I really wanted to hit a home run," I say, laughing.

"You're a good guy, Charlie. Most guys wouldn't even admit that," she says.

"You mean like your ex-boyfriend?" I say.

She takes her head off my shoulder and looks me in the eyes.

"You don't have to worry about any ex-boyfriends, Charlie."

She puts her head back on my shoulder.

Suddenly I get a great idea.

"Let's go see a movie," I say.

"Really?"

"Yeah. Just the two of us. Like a real date. Maybe that French one is still playing."

"Yeah," Miranda says. "Let's do it."

Of course I have no idea what they're saying and when

I read the subtitles I don't really know who is saying what, but still. It's fun. The music sounds pretty and the flowers are pretty and the French girl and boy certainly seem to be having fun and I'm so happy sharing my popcorn and soda with Miranda.

Since it's so cold in the theater, it's only natural to put my arm over Miranda's shoulders. And even though my arm falls asleep, there's no way in the world I'm moving it.

About halfway through the movie the boy and girl run off in a field of daffodils and fall into the flowers and have a real nice kiss. And not a gross one but a good one. If a kiss can say something, then that kiss was saying it's the first of many.

Miranda giggles a little bit and I look at her and she's still smiling. It feels great knowing that I make her happy, it really does. And that's when I lean over and kiss her on the cheek and she kisses me back and everything is perfect except for my arm, which I can't move on account of its falling asleep. But it doesn't matter. Nothing matters.

And when the popcorn falls on the floor, we both laugh. Billy was totally right about this film.

16

The Best Nite Ever!

SAM

I'm not overexaggerating when I say that Erica Dickerson could leave Penn Valley this second and go to New York and get a job writing for *Saturday Night Live*. In fact, when I get a free minute, I might write to Tina Fey and Mindy Kaling and tell them how talented Erica is.

And does she ever rock at NYC Nites.

But let me start at the beginning. When I walk into the lobby at school, I have to rub my eyes. I can't believe what I'm seeing. Although I've never been to an art gallery in New York City before, this has got to be exactly how it looks. The lobby is very bright and spotlights are shining on the paintings. I can't believe it. I really can't believe it.

And then I think I must be dreaming when I see Foxxy dressed in a blazer and some kind of scarf and a weird hat. This is the guy who is usually wearing dirty and ripped clothes with food stains.

Foxxy looks pretty serious, too, directing people on ladders to move the lights around. And there's a group of girls following him, telling him what a good artist he is. Wow. I mean, wow! I really want to see what all this is about, but I'm just a bit too nervous about emceeing, so I sneak down the side hallway to get to the backstage area of the auditorium.

For the first time, I begin to think we might be able to pull it off. Still, I'm so nervous about everything. I've never, ever, ever felt this way before. My mouth is so dry that I'm just downing bottles of water and then rushing off to the bathroom.

"Slow down there, Skippy," Erica says as I'm chugging about my seventeenth bottle of water.

I look at Erica, but I can't say anything.

"Are you nervous?"

I nod.

"We'll be all right. Trust me."

She hands me the call sheet, which is a list of all the acts that will be going up. I still can't believe it. I don't know how Erica did it, but she did. We have enough entertainment for a whole weekend, we really do.

Erica and I have some time to kill, since the art gallery and food station are first. We run through the call sheet and review our backup plans in case there's a problem. We also work with Richard Dansky, who's going to show the mall interview video we put together.

Before we know it, we're on. We only show one thing from the mall, which just happens to be me with pizza stuffed in my mouth. The crowd loves it, they absolutely love it.

From there it just takes off:

Sharon really nails a tap-dancing routine with Ralph Waldo. I heard she and Duke broke up, which is probably why they didn't do anything together. I can't say I'm not relieved. Duke is the worst!

Mr. Minkin, believe it or not, grabs the microphone and does a stand-up routine that I just can't believe. Who thought he had it in him. Here's just a sample of his jokes:

Mr. Minkin: The hardest thing about teaching is grading. I mean, it's really a lot of work. But then you have a kid like Foxxy. Every teacher gives him an A. There's no way a teacher is going to take the chance of having him for another year.

(I laugh pretty loud into my microphone.)

Mr. Minkin: What are you laughing at, Dolan? Why do you think you passed all your classes?

Boy, does that ever get the crowd going. And I don't even mind that he's ripping on me.

Next thing I know, Lichtensteiner's got the mic and is telling a story about the first day of school for many of us. He gets the whole crowd laughing when he tells about when he first met Duke Samagura and how Duke was upset because the library was closed. And how he gave Chollie Muller two detentions because he was late from playing football before school. And then he get the crowd roaring when he tells how he first met me and Foxxy when we couldn't stop laughing in Ms. Aguilar's class.

Then it hits me. This sounds exactly like what I wrote in Freewriting for Mr. Minkin's class. I look over at Mr. Minkin (who is laughing like crazy, by the way) and when Mr. Minkin sees me, he gives me a huge sly wink.

Can you believe that?!

But the best part of the night, at least for me, is being on the stage with Erica. She's such a natural. I seriously don't think I could do it, ever, without her. Emceeing together hurts less than I thought it would. I mean, my heart is broken and I wish Erica and I could get that feeling back, but it's okay, because I know she's my friend. And I'd rather be her friend than nothing at all.

CHOLLIE

It's funny, but until I really got to know Miranda I thought the whole world revolved around sports. Don't get me wrong, I still love sports and will try out for every team in high school, but Miranda just opens up my eyes to a whole new world.

As soon as Miranda and I get to NYC Nites, I just can't believe we were upset about not having the dance and the class trip. You can just feel this is way better than anything else because we all worked together to make something pretty amazing happen.

"This is awesome, Miranda. You did it," I say.

"*We* did it. Everyone helped. There are just a lot of procrastinators at Penn Valley, so it took a bit of time to put it all together."

She's got a big smile on her face, but I can tell she's still a little embarrassed about what happened at the student council meeting.

"You know, Miranda," I say, "that day when you went off on everyone, that really sparked the fire we needed."

"I don't think we need to revisit that episode," she says, but she's still smiling.

We have the best time watching all the acts on the talent stage. I had no idea Ralph Waldo could tap-dance, or that Terri McCool could juggle, or that Holly Culver could do magic. We really have a lot of talent at Penn Valley. Even the teachers are talented.

Halfway through the show Erica and Sam call up Miranda, and she announces that we raised more than five hundred dollars for the Penn Valley Vegetarian Society. Pretty cool, right?

After Miranda gets off the stage, we look at each other. And our eyes, when they meet, say so much. I don't know if she can see it, but my eyes say I couldn't have done it without her and I think she's the best thing in the whole wide world. I'm pretty sure her eyes say she's happy, and that's about all I need to know.

Miranda and I head over to the photo booth. I want to make sure I remember this night forever.

DUKE

The wonder of life is that we are continually learning.

I learned quite a lesson from Sharon Dolan that afternoon in the bookstore. After she discovered I was a fraud, we had a cup of coffee in the café and worked out the end of our relationship. Knuckles and Moose laughed at a nearby table and I didn't mind at all. I deserved it.

A lesser man would've feigned illness, or maybe just dropped out of school, but not Duke Vanderbilt Samagura. So despite my supreme disappointment at not giving the commencement speech and not having Sharon at my side, I found the strength to finish my sentence at Penn Valley. There I was in the lobby of the auditorium, checking in the crowd for NYC Nites.

Looking back on it now, it's truly remarkable we were able to pull it off. But I suppose it's a testament to the work I put in before the unfortunate events that kept me from my duties. I suppose Miranda, and really everyone, rose to the occasion as well.

The art of MiniMoMA was a hit. Everyone seemed to enjoy the grape juice. The cheese (lacking in variety) and crackers were consumed rather quickly. Jimmy Foxx, who has been a scourge of the education system for years, was actually wearing a beret (I was happy to see some of my style rub off on him) and leading groups to view the art. Who would've thought that could happen?

Everyone chipped in to pick up for the slackers on the food committee. We had quite a smorgasbord, really. Good old-fashioned American hot dogs. Pizzas, falafels, pupusas, and kreplach. In all, I counted at least sixteen countries represented, which is not all that New York City offers, but it wasn't bad for Penn Valley.

If you can believe it, Sam Dolan, who fancies himself some type of humorist, actually made me laugh with a joke about whether our principal exists. I myself have never seen her.

I watched as Sharon took the stage with Ralph Waldo. It was almost too much to endure, so I turned to the food carts for comfort.

It's funny how chance works. For at that very moment, I met the most wonderful, the most awe-inspiring, the most beautiful young woman my eyes had ever beheld.

I was trying the falafel, and some yoghurt slipped out from the pita. I stepped back, hoping it would not get on my suit and preparing to straighten out the falafel maker if it did.

"You don't want to get that on your bow tie." A mellifluous voice came from behind me.

I turned to see the most ravishing girl.

"So far so good," I said, checking my suit. "But of course I always carry a backup bow tie."

She chuckled, revealing her beautiful white teeth and perfect smile.

"Hi, I'm Portia," she said.

"It's a pleasure to meet you, Portia," I said, clasping her hand professionally, as if it were a business meeting. I was not going to overdo it this time.

"Forgive me, but I don't believe I've seen you at this school. Tell me about yourself."

"No need to apologize," she said. "I don't attend Penn Valley. I go to Cedarbrook. My mother's best friend has a son enrolled here. We've known each other our entire lives. Do you know Ralph Waldo? I think he's onstage right now."

"Is that so," I said. "So you're practically related," I added, for if it was not something she had thought of, I at least wanted to plant the seed. I felt instantly a need to protect this innocent rose from the lecherous Ralph Waldo.

"I wouldn't say that," she replied, laughing.

And what a laugh. What a smile. Her high cheekbones, lovely and firm, perfectly framed her bright brown eyes, and the light was perfect. She was absolutely stunning with her hair lit from behind by the setting sun. I don't know what music was playing in the auditorium, but in my mind I heard, I felt, Gershwin's "Rhapsody in Blue." There was so much potential, so much new in the world.

"Now tell me, Portia, will you be attending Penn Valley High School this fall?"

17

Freewriting

Chollie Muller

June 9, 2016

English 8A

Mr. Minkin

Suggested Writing Prompt: *If you were going to give a commencement speech, what would you say? What is the advice you'd give to younger students? Whom would you specifically thank? Who helped guide you through your years at Penn Valley Middle?*

Dear Mr. Minkin,

If I was lucky enough to give the commencement speech I think I'd start off thanking a whole lot of people. I guess my mom and dad first. They always get me up in the morning and my dad makes me breakfast and

my mom makes my lunch. That's pretty cool of
them and I've never thanked them. So I guess I
would thank them during the commencement
speech. And now that I think about it I should
probably thank them tonight.

My brother Billy should also be thanked.
Though truthfully, his advice almost made me
lose my girlfriend multiple times. But he gets
an "A" for effort. And besides, he's always been
there for me.

I think I'd be able to give young people
advice, too. One piece of advice would be to
hold the football with two hands until you cross
the goal line. And practice your free throws.
You'll never know when you'll be standing
there all alone at the free throw line with two
shots to win the game. And believe in yourself,
because if you give up you'll never know what
you can accomplish. No matter what, you
gotta stick with it. Look at us. We finally won a
championship. And I have to admit even though
I wanted to hit a homer to win the game, being a
good teammate is a pretty great feeling, and just
as important as anything else.

Last but not least, I think I'd like to thank Miranda. There's just something about her. When I'm with her I feel on top of the world and also very relaxed at the same time. Without Miranda I just know I would not have gotten that bunt down in the baseball game. I almost think without Miranda I wouldn't have had any fun this semester, if you can believe that.

So even though I'm excited for high school and happy Miranda and I will be going to Penn Valley High together, there are lots of things I'm going to miss about middle school.

Hey, Mr. Minkin! If you notice a little something on the paper it's teardrops. How about that?

Duke Vanderbilt Samagura

9 June 2016

English 8A

Mr. Minkin

Suggested Writing Prompt: *If you were going to give a commencement speech, what would you say? What is the advice you'd give to younger students? Whom would you specifically thank? Who helped guide you through your years at Penn Valley Middle?*

Sir:

Now that I've seen your stand-up comedy routine, I'm beginning to have an entirely different view of you.

Before NYC Nites I would have accused you of twisting the knife Lichtensteiner stuck in my back by picking names out of a hat instead of having a fair competition for the speech. But now I realize that you have a sense of humor, albeit a sick one.

Perhaps you should pack your bags and bring your talents to Penn Valley High. I'm sure you can't be worse than who's currently teaching there.

At any rate, I must say I'm glad I'm not giving the commencement speech. What I had prepared was a speech based on Pericles' extolling the glory of Greece. Thinking back on it, it may have been a trifle boring. And based upon the lessons Sharon taught me, it might not have been appropriate for the occasion. After all, we're only moving ahead to the ninth grade. Pericles was giving the eulogy to fallen soldiers who gave their lives to Athens.

Keeping that in mind, perhaps your questions would make for a better commencement speech. I would advise the younger students to fight for their right to a first-rate education. I'm certain the school will try to cut the library's hours once I'm gone. Don't let them. The library is yours.

I would advise younger students to push Mr. Wexler into taking chances with theatre. Theatre is alive! It is protean! It is necessary for a functioning democracy.

I would tell the students that the student council is a powerful tool. And I would tell them to remember NYC Nites, to never forget how we, the class of 2016, took the bad news of the canceled class trip and pulled off a night to remember.

Who would I thank? Is that your bid, Mr. Minkin, to get an undeserved mention, a "shout-out" as they say, in a bogus commencement speech? If that is the case, you will be disappointed, for I shall not thank you.

And I won't thank Mr. Lichtensteiner, who runs the school the way Knuckles and Moose would, if they had a chance to run a school.

And I won't thank my parents, Neal and Cassandra, who are too interested in their books and their college students to worry about me. Then again, maybe I should thank them for letting me, Duke Vanderbilt Samagura, be me.

Erica Dickerson

June 9, 2016

English 8A

Mr. Minkin

Suggested Writing Prompt: *If you were going to give a commencement speech, what would you say? What is the advice you'd give to younger students? Whom would you specifically thank? Who helped guide you through your years at Penn Valley Middle?*

If I was going to write a commencement speech, Mr. Minkin, I don't think I'd prepare for it. You know how sometimes when you hear a speech you can tell that it's been memorized and over-rehearsed and it comes out sounding insincere? That's not what I would want for my speech. Sometimes the best moments are improvised.

In fact, that is exactly how I would begin my commencement speech. I started as a new kid without knowing a single soul, and now I have friends who I hope will always be at my side.

I would advise the younger students in the crowd to try new things, whether it's going out for the play or a sports team or working on the yearbook. It's probably where you'll make great friends and have more fun than anywhere else at Penn Valley.

And I would warn younger students to stay away from the turkey with the yellow gravy. Why is the gravy yellow? It looks like it's radioactive.

And I'd suggest always carrying some extra toilet paper. You never know when a toilet paper rebellion will break out, so you can never be too prepared.

In all seriousness, I would encourage younger students to laugh every day, and not be afraid to cry when you have to, even if you have to do it alone in your room after you make a tough decision. And when you're done, pick yourself up and start a new day.

Sam Dolan

June 9th 2016

English 8A

Mr. Minkin

Suggested Writing Prompt: *If you were going to give a commencement speech, what would you say? What is the advice you'd give to younger students? Whom would you specifically thank? Who helped guide you through your years at Penn Valley Middle?*

Hey Mr. Minkin,

Not only would I thank a whole bunch of people, but I would also like to leave them with something. Nothing huge, just a little something to remember me and the Class of 2016. And since I'm still a couple of years away from making millions, I'm going to leave IOUs.

To Mr. Minkin: A book of writing prompts. This way you can be sure you'll never run out of questions to ask your students.

To Mr. Lichtensteiner: A huge signed portrait of me to hang in his office. He always gave me a hard time, but I have a feeling he's going to miss me.

To Mr. Porter: A gavel so he can keep order at the student council meetings. Seriously, Miranda and Duke really did all of the work.

To Mrs. Stempen: A tracking system so students can never smuggle dissected frog parts from the lab. I doubt Foxxy and I are the only ones who have ever thought of that. We might be the only ones who thought to put the parts on lunch trays as a joke, though.

And to my friends, I owe them so much. But mostly I need to thank them.

To Foxxy: I need to thank Foxxy for being a good guy to me after Erica dumped me. Can you believe I almost didn't show up for the NYC Nites celebration? It just goes to show what a good friend he is, especially after I sort of treated him bad after Holly Culver broke up with him. I owe Foxxy big time for also making just about every day at Penn Valley great fun.

To my younger sister Sharon: I hope she's watched me closely so she doesn't make the same mistakes I did. She's already made a great decision by breaking up with Duke. So she'll probably be fine next year.

To Erica Dickerson: I would just say thanks to Erica. If I haven't told her, I'd want her to know she made the end of Penn Valley Middle School more fun than I could have ever dreamed. I hope we'll stay friends in high school.

Miranda Mullaly

June 9, 2016

English 8A

Mr. Minkin

Suggested Writing Prompt: *If you were going to give a commencement speech, what would you say? What is the advice you'd give to younger students? Whom would you specifically thank? Who helped guide you through your years at Penn Valley Middle?*

If I were going to give the commencement speech, I don't think I would give any advice to younger students. Those younger students probably won't heed my advice anyway and, hopefully, they'll be making the same mistakes all of us did. Looking back on my years here, I don't think I would've had any fun if I didn't make mistakes. I mean, flipping out at the student council meeting was the most embarrassing thing I've ever done. I could barely bring myself to go to school the next day. Now, I'm smiling at myself just thinking about it. It set some wonderful things in motion.

And I don't think I'd go through a list thanking people. Not unless I wanted to put everyone in the crowd to sleep.

I think if I was going to give the commencement speech it would be short, like this freewriting exercise. I've learned to stop overthinking things.

I would say eat your veggies, study for tests, be the first in line in the cafeteria when they have tater tots.

Oh, and have fun, because it goes by really, really fast.

Jake Gerhardt

was born and raised in Cheltenham, Pennsylvania. He attended Elkins Park Middle School, where he played football and basketball, ran track, performed in the school musical, and was a member of the student council. He also found time to attend many school dances, in constant pursuit of a (future ex-) girlfriend.

Since graduating from West Chester University, he has worked as a teacher. He currently lives in Los Angeles with his pulchritudinous wife and two amazing daughters.

Jake is the author of *Me and Miranda Mullaly* and *My Future Ex-Girlfriend*. Please visit him at jakegerhardt.com.